HER SECRET, HIS SURPRISE

Conflict of interest is an understatement...

Since being disowned by her strict father, Cass Stone has spent her adulthood trying to prove him wrong. Her drive has led to more success than her family ever thought she'd achieve, and life is looking great. Not even an incredible and mysterious one night stand that leaves her a single mom can trip her up...until the father of her baby stumbles back into her life, as sexy and unreliable as ever.

Logan Alexander hasn't forgotten the night he spent with Cass two years ago, but he never expects to end up undercover as her assistant. His job saves lives—like it should have saved his brother—and he can't afford complications. It's difficult enough to maintain his cover as a carefree wanderer when he realizes his attraction to Cass hasn't faded...and then he meets Cass's daughter.

Her Secret, His Surprise

PAULA ALTENBURG

This book is a work of fiction. Names, characters, places, and incidents are the product of the author's imagination or are used fictitiously. Any resemblance to actual events, locales, or persons, living or dead, is coincidental.

Copyright © 2014 by Paula Altenburg All rights reserved, including the right to reproduce, distribute, or transmit in any form or by any means. For information regarding subsidiary rights, please contact the Publisher.

Entangled Publishing, LLC
2614 South Timberline Road
Suite 109
Fort Collins, CO 80525
Visit our website at www.entangledpublishing.com.

Bliss is an imprint of Entangled Publishing, LLC. For more information on our titles, visit http://www.entangledpublishing.com/category/bliss

Edited by Kerri-Leigh Grady and Jessica Snyder
Cover design by Jessica Cantor

Print ISBN   978-1-50098-009-2

Manufactured in the United States of America

First Edition July 2014

*To Jessica Snyder and Kerri-Leigh Grady.
Thank you.*

Chapter One

Cassiopeia Stone blinked a little behind her black-framed glasses as the alcohol settled in her stomach and spread relaxing warmth through her limbs.

The hotel bar was dark, deserted, and smelled a bit funky. Like a few too many beer had slopped over the tops of overfull steins. The atmosphere was intimate, and the tables secluded enough for private conversation.

In other words, based on her limited experience, it was fairly typical of conference hotel bars.

"We've held the Canadian first- and second-line maintenance manuals contract on P-3 aircraft for the past twenty-seven years, and were one of the first Canadian contractors to bring interactive electronic manuals into service. We continue to innovate," Cass heard herself babble. "We use the same software providers your company does. If you decide to use Kramer Aerospace's publications department on your upcoming contract, you won't be sorry,

Mr. Finder."

"I'm sure I won't be," the colonel murmured. "Please. Call me Chris." Under the table, he dropped his hand to her nylon-clad thigh. "Perhaps we could take this back to my room."

Cass knew how she would have handled this situation when she was sixteen. At twenty-five, and in a business environment, she chose to be more circumspect. It was a shame that Christopher Finder, who had to be at least seventy, seemed to have a thing for younger women—along with a wide strip of ego—because this was where she drew the line. She wasn't sleeping with him. Not even to score a multimillion dollar contract.

"I won't take up much more of your time. I promise, I only have a few more slides."

She inched away from the colonel's groping fingers, then knocked back her drink maybe faster than was prudent. The next business trip she took, she told herself, she wasn't getting her fashion advice from the company vice president's executive assistant. Maxine always looked so elegant, but now Cass knew beyond a doubt that a business suit would have been far more appropriate for the national defense conference than high heels and a short skirt.

Crooking one long, corkscrew curl behind her ear with an index finger, she moved on to the next slide of her PowerPoint presentation. She nudged the laptop around so the retired lieutenant colonel could get a look at the screen and stop staring down the front of her blouse.

She'd come to this conference to staff the exhibit booth for Kramer Aerospace and Defence, and landed a private pitch with the vice president of international business development for one of the major North American aerospace defense companies. She had her eye on a director's position at Kramer Aerospace that was opening up in a few years. Bringing in a new contract for that department would fast-track her for promotion.

The colonel eyed the half-empty glass on the small round table in front of Cass, then raised a hand to signal for the cute bartender to bring them two more.

She didn't protest. She simply told herself to slow down. She was nervous and eager, not stupid, and while her new friend Chris might be an old lecher, she had no real concerns about her personal safety.

What she did have was serious angst as to how this meeting might be recapped later if things didn't turn out the way the colonel would like. Her boss had taken a risk by sending her to this conference in his place, and she wanted him to know that his faith in her hadn't been a mistake. She needed to wrap up her presentation with some semblance of professionalism.

A ringtone pealed out "Baby Love" by the Supremes, loud in the empty room. The colonel pulled his phone from a pocket and checked the number displayed. He frowned. "Excuse me a moment. I have to take this call."

He edged his squat wooden chair away from the low pedestal table, scraping it across the funky carpeting so he could stand. Cass breathed easier as he disappeared in the direction of the foyer and men's room.

The bartender brought their drinks. Her brain was foggy enough by now that, when combined with her relief that the presentation was almost done, and the conference was over, the smile she gave him as he settled her drink in front of her

was extra-high wattage.

"Enjoying the conference?" he asked, smiling back at her, deep indigo eyes dancing as if they were sharing a private joke. He added a wink for good measure.

Cass met his eyes and read unconcealed interest. She had to admit, she was floored. The man was beautiful. He wore his dark, tousled hair a bit long and brushed away from a high-cheek-boned face in a surfer-dude style. Laugh lines bracketed a wide mouth. If he'd been the one plying her with drinks, she wouldn't think twice about taking her pitch somewhere more private.

She was riding a bit of a high right now, which brought out an innate recklessness that she knew from experience could swing either way for her. She'd always liked to take risks and was quick to seize opportunities. It had gotten her disowned by her father when she was eighteen. It had also gotten her scholarships and an engineering degree without any help from the unforgiving bastard.

That evil inner voice nudged her, the one that pushed her to take risks and sometimes got her in trouble. It said she was a two-hour plane ride from home. No one would know what she did. It also reminded her of the three condoms in her purse that had been there for so long they were due to expire.

While the bartender was worth checking out, he'd undoubtedly been hit on enough in his line of work that he'd know exactly what was up, and that irked her a bit. She didn't like being seen as a cliché.

Then again, she didn't have to care what his impression of her might be, no matter how cute he was. Let him think what he liked. She'd never see him again. Besides, he could always say no if he wasn't interested. She had a darned good position with a prestigious company. Years of hard work were paying off, and she wanted to celebrate.

"It's been a long week. I'm about ready to unwind," she replied. "But I hate mixing business with pleasure."

The colonel reappeared, tucking his phone back in his suit jacket pocket as he strode toward them.

Cass gave the good-looking bartender another lift of her lips meant to convey an interest on her part as well, and then she turned back to the colonel, her drink, and the tail end of a presentation she could hardly wait to be over.

• • •

Logan Alexander knew when he'd been dismissed.

He tried not to laugh, but she made it hard. He earned his living by reading people, and traffic had been light in the bar all evening so he'd spent most of the past hour watching her work. The pretty little professional playing dress-up seemed to think the black-rimmed glasses she wore made men take her more seriously.

If that was her intention, she should have done something about her hair, too, because the only serious thing her tangle of long, golden-brown ringlets whispered was *sexy librarian*. She'd done her best to fasten it all back with some sort of fancy gold clip, but instead, managed to look more like she'd just crawled out of bed.

That turned her into a sleepy, sexy librarian.

In reality, Logan suspected she was the company eye candy, probably junior management level, sent here to pretty up an otherwise generic display booth. She'd been attending the annual Canadian Defence Industry conference, or the "See-Dicks," as he liked to call it. That was because the conference was full of dickheads.

Since he'd nailed one of them to the wall that afternoon, he was feeling pretty damned good. By day, he worked for the Canadian Security Intelligence Service. He'd filed his final report to his CSIS superiors and technically, the case he'd been following was now closed. Most of the conference attendees were gone and the hotel was quiet.

He liked tending bar, so he'd offered to finish out this last shift before the regular bartender returned from "vacation."

Besides, right now Miss Professional was making a sales pitch to a retired light colonel who was only interested in what was inside that silky white blouse, not her PowerPoint presentation, and it was like watching a train wreck unfolding in slow motion. She had no idea the guy she was trying to impress didn't have any buying power. The retired colonel was one of the many ringers private companies hired to send to these functions so they could schmooze up any important contacts they had left over from their military careers. The real meetings happened away from the actual conference. She was wasting her time.

So was the colonel. He'd never get her drunk enough to score. Miss Professional, although young, was wise to that plan. It also appeared as if she could hold her liquor.

Logan had made it easier for her. The drink he'd passed her was virgin. He watched her take a small, cautious sip.

Her gaze cut to the bar over the rim of her glass. For a second, a slight smile of acknowledgment licked at the corners of her full lips before disappearing.

He relaxed. She had a good sense of humor. Not to

mention, self-preservation.

She was also adorable. If he had to guess he'd say she'd once been a rebellious teen seeking her daddy's attention, then turned her life around before too much damage was done—possibly with the intervention of a private school for wayward teenagers. But that was a guess.

He'd bet he had the *rebellious teen* part right though, and that she wasn't so far past those years she'd forgotten what they felt like. She had a reckless streak in her, or she wouldn't be having drinks with the colonel.

The meeting wrapped up. The colonel, realizing he wasn't going to get what he wanted, passed Miss Professional his business card with a press of his palm to hers and an overlong handshake.

To Logan's acute disappointment, Miss Professional left the bar without a backward glance. The colonel made a phone call, most likely to his wife, judging by his abrupt change in manner. Then he left, too.

And there went Logan's entertainment for the evening. He started to clean up the empty bar, wiping down tables and straightening chairs.

Miss Professional returned half an hour later, wearing tight jeans that clung to long legs and a white T-shirt emblazoned with a company logo. She was tall, probably close to five ten, and at six foot three himself, Logan liked that in a woman. The mass of light brown ringlets was loose now, draping over her shoulders and spilling down her back.

He had to admit, he found those curls sexy as hell. He could imagine his fingers all caught up in them, his naked body pressed to hers, those long legs wrapped around his hips…

He grinned as she walked up to the bar where he leaned against the gleaming surface. The black-framed glasses were gone. She had wide, hazel eyes with long, gold-tipped lashes that brushed her cheeks whenever she dropped her gaze.

Right now, her gaze was direct. She smiled right back at him. Every predatory instinct he owned went on red alert.

"Is it too late to order another mojito?" she asked.

"Not at all. Virgin?" He reached for a glass.

She blinked, those lashes fluttering up and down. "What?"

He held up the glass. "Your mojito? Would you like this one with or without alcohol in it?"

She laughed, her eyes dancing with fun and happiness at the shared joke, and he was completely, 100 percent smoked.

"With, please."

She was celebrating. Since he knew the colonel wasn't in a position to offer her anything business-related she'd be this excited about, it had to be something else.

Something that mattered to her. A lot.

He could identify. He felt like celebrating, too. His job was to investigate the activities of the Canadian Department of National Defence's maintenance contractors. The dickhead he'd nailed had sold off an entire inventory of aging weapons systems—meaning aircraft that could be turned into bombers—to a third-world country with nuclear capabilities. Illegal on so many levels, not to mention completely lacking in morality. The guy had no doubt thought that by selling the aircraft in pieces he wasn't breaking any federal laws. Or at the very least, had managed to circumvent them.

Logan's brother-in-law had been shot down over Afghanistan, on what was meant to be a peacekeeping mission, because some bureaucrat like this had gotten greedy. Six soldiers lost. Nine children left without fathers, his two young nephews included. People handed a little authority could turn into such self-entitled assholes sometimes, with no regard for the consequences to others.

Yet this guy he'd tagged today had been only one link in a very long, complicated chain. The customer who'd bought those weapons systems remained active, and as yet, unidentified.

Frustrating.

He flipped the switch on the blender. When the drink was ready he poured it into a glass, added the garnish, and passed it over with a flourish. Then he reached across the bar and offered her his hand.

"Logan," he said.

"M-M-Mary," she stuttered as she took it in hers. "M-Mary Smith."

She sucked at lying. That intrigued him even more. First, because she was bad at it, and he'd assumed she'd be more of a pro. Second, because she felt the need to lie to him about her real name.

She was slumming.

With anyone else, he would have backed off at this point. He didn't mind the slumming. Being invisible was part of his job. He had no time to pursue permanent relationships with women who needed impressing.

But she'd had a few drinks. She was here on business. And she was celebrating something. In his experience, that often led to reckless decisions that they'd both end up regretting later. He didn't like liars either, not in his line of work, but with M-M-Mary, it qualified more as withholding the truth. Plus he was working, too. Officially, even though the report had been passed in, he was still on the CSIS clock. He'd need to show up at the office for debriefing first thing in the morning.

But Miss Mary Professional Smith possessed an odd mix of innocence and adventure that he found more than a little appealing, and she had fun in her eyes. She didn't want to celebrate whatever it was alone, and for some reason, had decided he was safe. She wasn't reckless so much as spontaneous, and she'd sized him up right. All the next moves would have to be hers.

He was curious how many more she was willing to make.

...

The drink hit Cass harder than she'd anticipated, probably because of the three she'd had earlier in the day.

That wasn't going to change her mind about tonight. She was a good judge of character. It had kept her out of jail as a teen. If Logan hadn't slid her that first virgin drink, she wouldn't be here right now, sounding him out. She found his quiet confidence attractive. She liked his smile, and the way he didn't try to pretend not to know what she was after. He also didn't put on any pressure.

She was in charge.

The drink merely served to relax her.

"What are you celebrating?" he asked.

She ran her finger around the rim of her glass and fidgeted on the bar stool, surprised by the astuteness of the question. She prided herself on being more difficult to read than this. "What makes you think I have something to celebrate?"

"You give off a happy, self-satisfied vibe. While my ego's healthy enough, I'm pretty sure it's not all thanks to me."

She wiped her damp palms on her thighs. This was a hookup, nothing more. She didn't want to share any details of her life with him. She wasn't after a relationship. She liked who she was and where she was in her life, but every once in a while, it was nice to pretend to be someone else. Something different. This was the perfect opportunity. And the right guy.

She might as well go for outrageous in answer to his question. She'd stumbled over the fake name, and there was no way he hadn't noticed because he didn't seem stupid. Besides, she'd picked the lamest one imaginable. She could blame that much on the alcohol.

"I just got out of prison," she said. She let out a dramatic sigh as she braced her elbow on the bar and planted her chin in her palm. "You have no idea what a relief it is to finally meet a good-looking man who isn't dressed in a Corrections Canada uniform."

His eyes lit up like twin blue lasers as he played along. "Good-looking, huh? What were you in for?"

"Overenthusiasm with a bullwhip and handcuffs. Something might have been mentioned about 'inflicting permanent physical and emotional scars on the victim.'"

He sniffed in disgust. "The guy was a sissy if he couldn't handle a little domination."

She drained the last of her drink and slid the empty glass across the bar toward him. She lifted her chin, sat up straight on the stool, and met those twin laser beams head-on. "Who says it was a guy?"

"Now I'm intrigued." He took the glass but didn't offer her another. Instead, he got out the fountain gun and filled two tall tumblers with club soda and ice. He passed her one, then tapped the bottom of his to the side of hers. "Cheers. Good luck staying straight with your probation."

"Thanks."

Logan, his sweating tumbler in one long-fingered hand, leaned against the counter behind him, facing her where she perched at the bar. He had a faint scruff of dark stubble shading his jaw that looked like it might be a teensy bit scratchy on delicate skin. His shirtsleeves were rolled back to expose a small flag tattooed on the inside of one well-muscled forearm. She could see his reflection from behind in the row of mirrors that lined the wall behind the rows of liquor bottles. No bald spots.

She swirled the cubes of ice, watching them jockey for position between the bubbles of soda, and fed him an easy one-liner. "Why did you make me a virgin earlier?"

He didn't respond with the sexual innuendo she'd set him up for. Instead, he shrugged.

"I don't like men who ply uninterested women with alcohol, hoping to gain an advantage."

Cass was charmed because he sounded so sincere. The guy really was hot, and on more than one level. "What if she's interested and he's already got an advantage?"

He saluted her with the half-empty glass of club soda. "Then alcohol wouldn't be necessary, now, would it?"

"For the record, the virgin wasn't necessary either. I can take care of myself."

"Since we're stating things for the record," he replied, those laser-blue eyes warm and steady on hers, "you wouldn't have to worry about safety with me."

That was the opening she'd been waiting for. She leaned on the bar, bringing herself into his personal space and within easy batting range. She gave him her best smile. "I think you're safe enough."

He set his drink down. He stepped up to the plate. And he stroked the pad of one finger along the length of her cheek to the underside of her chin before tipping her face upward. His answering smile was way better than hers. Her insides swirled.

"There's only one way to find out," he said.

And she was going to take it.

A jolt of anticipation exploded through Cass, along with a vestige of common sense. She was a sucker for risk taking, but she wasn't a gambler. She wasn't dumb either. Not when it came to her future. She didn't want to be seen crossing the lobby and entering an elevator with him. She had no idea who from the conference might still be here, if they had any connection to her company, or if they might recognize her later. If she'd learned anything in life, it was to cover her ass.

She had two entry key cards for her room.

"Do you personally return items that are left at the bar, or do you hand them in at the desk?" she asked.

"It depends on the item." His grin, sexy and slow, dampened her panties. "And who left it behind."

She took one of the key cards from her back pocket and dropped it onto the bar between them. Then she spread all of her cards on the table.

"Room 2014. My flight leaves at ten in the morning. I'll have to be out of here before eight."

...

Two months later, as Cass sat on her bathroom floor with her head hanging over the toilet bowl, she was forced to acknowledge that condoms probably had expiry dates for a reason. Her purse, a catchall for dry pens and other junk with sharp edges, might not have been the safest place to store them either.

She'd had quite the celebration that night. All she'd wanted was a fun time and a memory. It seemed she'd gotten more than she'd bargained for.

Logan was going to be really hard to forget now.

When the dry heaves finally ended, she sat back on the cold white tiles and rested her sweaty forehead on her knees, wondering what she should do, and too tired to think.

She knew she should try to reach him and at least tell him he was going to be a father, and reassure him she had no expectations, only thought he should know. She had a good job and didn't need child support. No way could he afford it on a bartender's tips. She wouldn't do that to him.

She closed her eyes. Her baby's father was a bartender. Her own, a minister with rigid beliefs, would have a stroke if he knew. But hers would never find out because he'd cut all ties a long time ago and made it clear that no one else in the family was to speak to her either. None of her sisters, or her mother, had ever dared disobey him.

Cass was the lone rebel. The black sheep.

She'd been on her own for more than seven years now. She'd made a good life for herself. She had a few close college friends she could trust, but they were scattered around the country. She never discussed her personal life at work, so no one there would ever know that this pregnancy was the result of a one-night stand.

The best one night of her life.

Logan had been everything she'd expected and then some. Funny, sweet, smart…and gone before she woke up in the morning, so things hadn't ended on an awkward note. She hated to screw up the memories for either one of them by contacting him now, but her conscience wouldn't allow her to keep this to herself.

She struggled through the workday, and when four thirty arrived, stumbled back to her apartment to grab a nap on her couch before dinner.

At eight o'clock in the evening, she braced herself and called the bar at the conference hotel. She asked for Logan, and after a lengthy pause, was told she must have the wrong number. Her fingers tightened around her cellphone, causing the volume button to chirp in her ear. Vegetable soup and whole-wheat crackers swirled in her stomach, threatening a comeback.

"He worked there two months ago," she insisted.

There was another long stretch of silence. She heard hushed voices as people conferred in the background. Then she was told that they didn't know of anyone by that name who'd ever worked for them. She hung up the phone, both terrified and relieved. Once again, she was all on her own.

But she wouldn't be alone for much longer.

She made a mad dash for the bathroom and spent the rest of the night throwing up.

Chapter Two

Two years later

"Someone in your company is selling military secrets."

Logan sat back and waited to see how the man with the thinning blond hair and wearing the five-thousand-dollar suit, seated behind the heavy mahogany desk would take that announcement.

Quite well, all things considered. Baxter Dempsey didn't show real surprise, which told Logan he'd at least suspected he had a problem.

That ticked Logan off. Perhaps the classified government publications Kramer Aerospace and Defence produced as part of their maintenance contract weren't top secret, but their handling still fell under the Canadian Security Intelligence Service's jurisdiction.

CSIS took a dim view of traitors.

Logan pretended to study the toe of one sneaker, noting

how Dempsey tried hard to hide the worry in his eyes but couldn't quite pull it off.

"At least no one will be getting rich off it," Dempsey finally said.

"CSIS would really rather be able to say that no one will be getting killed because of it," he replied. "Those NATO publications were meant for a summit meeting. When the position of deployed naval vessels is leaked ahead of time, there's a good chance at least one of those ships is going to end up as a hostile's target."

Dempsey blew out a sigh. His gaze met Logan's. "So do you have any idea who the leak might be?"

"We're looking first at people with direct access to the publications, then anyone living beyond their means," Logan said, careful to keep his own expression and tone neutral. Was Dempsey's concern for himself, for the company, or for someone else entirely?

Because it certainly wasn't for the servicemen on those ships. They were faceless. Anonymous. People like Logan were their only protection in situations like this one, and he took his job very seriously.

It was the least he could do to honor the memory of his sister's husband. Servicemen—and women—needed to know that their government had their backs.

He let Dempsey think about it for a bit. He looked through the office window at the shining waters of the Halifax Harbour, and the ferry chugging its way toward the Dartmouth shoreline on the other side. His work took him all over the world, and he'd been thinking a lot lately about setting up a home base somewhere. He'd seriously considered Toronto to be close to his parents, and his sister and her two kids, but he'd been dragging his heels on that. He'd grown up in a small town outside of Halifax and his grandmother was here. Although it had been a few years since he'd been back to Nova Scotia, and more than twenty since he'd lived here, no matter how long he stayed away, this still felt like home to him.

But he'd probably choose Toronto. His nephews were monsters. Someone needed to keep them out of jail.

"If you're looking for people living beyond their means, that could be anyone in upper management," Dempsey said.

Logan dragged his attention back to the man seated across from him. "Upper management is more likely to be stealing from the company than the company's customers."

The corner of Dempsey's mouth kicked up a fraction. "I wish I could deny that."

He tapped his desk with the tips of his fingers, letting Logan know that he was taking this far more seriously than he let on, and Logan relaxed.

He was in.

"Okay." Dempsey blew out a sigh. "How can I help?"

...

Most people started their New Year's resolutions on January first. Cass chose the end of the old fiscal year.

She wished she could claim it was because she dared to be different. In actual fact, it was because her current tax bill meant she and Olivia could forget any more renovations for a long while.

Cass liked being outside the city. Cornwall was a pretty, friendly little town and only a short drive from downtown

Halifax. But owning an old house in a nice neighborhood had proven more costly than anticipated.

She tapped the long envelope against her top lip a few times before forcing herself to insert it into the mail slot. She heard the faint whisper of paper hitting bottom. Taxes were the government equivalent of a catch-and-release program. She got to look at the money, maybe play with it a little. But sooner or later, she had to let it go. Today was the big day. The fact that the sun was shining and it was her birthday simply added insult to injury.

She blew a burnt-honey-streaked curl off her forehead and turned on one heel, wobbling a little on the cracked sidewalk, and headed toward the new minivan parked in the paved driveway of the stately old home she'd bought the year before. It was a fixer-upper, which translated to "money pit," but she'd fallen in love with the house, the town, and the neighbors, pretty much in that order. Her two-story house sat on a large corner lot sporting enormous lilac and rosebushes on its front lawn, and several ancient oaks in the backyard. She pictured that yard filled with toys, tree houses, and a gigantic, stainless-steel barbecue.

Best of all, there was a daycare within walking distance. She'd already dropped seventeen-month-old Olivia off for the day, kissing her daughter goodbye on her soft, ringlet-covered head before prying herself loose so she could head to the office.

The daycare did have a downside. Cass had never considered herself all that traditional until she'd met some of the other mothers and fielded a few nosy, personal questions about her marital status and family. The pity she'd seen in their eyes hit her hard, because she didn't need it.

Still, because of those questions, a month ago she'd decided her mother, at least, deserved to know she was a grandmother to this wonderful, beautiful little bundle that filled her own heart with so much love and joy. Cass had gotten a brief note back from her father instead.

You and your bastard are to stay away from my family.

No one called Olivia a bastard. Cass could dodge nosy questions, but what would happen when Olivia started school and had to face them, too?

She shouldn't have to answer for choices Cass made.

So Cass had begun giving serious, preemptive consideration to dating again and finding Olivia a father. One who could help pay the bills, because Cornwall, and the house, were nonnegotiable.

Maybe it was time to check out that online dating service a friend had suggested.

Look on the bright side, she thought as she got in the minivan and stuck her key in the ignition. At least she and Olivia had a beautiful old house and a brand-spanking new ride.

A new vehicle was no good to her if it wouldn't start.

She rested her chin against the steering wheel, flicking the key ring dangling from the ignition with one French-manicured fingernail. She'd only had the minivan out of the driveway three times, and now the stupid piece of plastic-coated, reinforced steel wouldn't budge. Maybe she shouldn't have bought it new but she'd needed something safe and reliable, with plenty of seating. She liked taking her elderly neighbors for their weekly groceries. They were sweet, and they loved spending time with Olivia.

Besides, in her company it was necessary to look successful, and this new promotion wouldn't be officially hers until her probationary period was over in another three months. She could drive a minivan, but she couldn't drive junk.

Right now she couldn't drive this heap of scrap metal at all.

Hazel eyes laced with irritation stared back at her from the rearview mirror. If she couldn't get it to start, she was going to be late for work, and that was one thing she hated. As a single mother, people already expected her to take advantage of her position as acting director and show up in the mornings at her personal convenience. A professional had to be prepared for these random acts of chance.

At least this random act was under warranty.

She grabbed her briefcase and her iPhone. Public transit was out. The city bus only ran every half hour out here in the county, and she'd never make it to the stop on time wearing heels. She slammed the van door a little too hard.

A gray head and pair of bright blue eyes popped over the dew-tipped hedge separating their properties.

"You need a man."

Normally Cass enjoyed talking to her neighbor. This morning she wasn't in the mood for cheerful optimism.

She plastered on a smile.

"Good morning, Mrs. Sheridan," she called, ignoring her neighbor's observation.

"If you had a man, he could get your car started for you," the elderly woman persisted.

Cass was an engineer by training. She could no doubt figure out what the problem was if she had the time, but she'd still need a diagnostics run on the van's computer and a mechanic to fix it. "It's okay. The van's under warranty."

"You should meet my grandson. He's coming to live with me. He could get your car started for you. He's a nice boy."

"Boy" meant he could be any age between eighteen and forty-nine, not that it mattered. Cass was highly suspicious of a grown man who lived with his grandmother. And come to think of it, she'd never heard Mrs. Sheridan speak of him before. Cass smelled a loser.

"What does your grandson do?" she asked, curious now. Maybe he was moving in because his grandmother needed someone to look after her. Mrs. Sheridan had always seemed self-sufficient to her, but at the same time she was no judge of the elderly. From what she could tell on their weekly excursions, they were all individual.

There was a split second of hesitation.

"He's a nice boy," Mrs. Sheridan repeated before her head disappeared behind the hedge.

Which meant he was probably bringing three computers and a gaming system with him and would spend all his time locked in the basement, building a dot.com empire and earning online gaming points for wealthy Asians.

No thanks.

Cass swallowed the cost, called a cab, and made it to the office with twenty minutes to spare.

"Hi," she greeted the gray-haired commissionaire behind the security desk as she flashed him her pass.

"Hey, Cass," he returned. A smile puckered his lined face as he buzzed her in. "How's the new job going?"

"Great. Wonderful."

Her answering smile wobbled a bit. Walking through the front doors felt like trading one set of problems for another. She'd begged her boss for the chance to prove she could run this department despite her young age and a year's worth of maternity leave. She'd been back in the office for five months now and thought this might be the one obstacle in her so-far-skyrocketing career that she might not be able to hurdle.

Part of it had a lot to do with her staff's negative attitudes. They all seemed to have one speed. Off. *I'll get it done when I get it done* was becoming a standard response to her requests for updates on projects. And if one more person muttered the word *micromanager* behind her back again, she was going to lose it completely. No court in the land would convict her.

Cranky old men. That was what she'd saddled herself with. Most of them were retired military who hadn't heard that somewhere between the seventeenth century and the twenty-first women had earned the right to vote. Not one of them took her promotion to acting director seriously. It didn't help that the average employee's age was about nine hundred compared to her twenty-seven.

The elevator rumbled to a stop at her floor. She groped in her briefcase for her keys, then a few minutes later, was annoyed to discover that her office had been left unlocked. Again.

This was supposed to be a secure building. Couldn't the cleaning staff think to lock a simple door behind them?

She checked the other doors on the floor and noticed that the closet for the classified publications was unlocked as well. She was going to have to speak to the supervisors.

She didn't care how many jokes people cracked about North Koreans giving back Canadian military secrets because they weren't worth the paper they were printed on. This was a secure building. That door was supposed to be locked at all times.

She grabbed the stack of papers from her in-box on the administrative assistant's desk and headed back to her office.

At nine o'clock she noticed the admin assistant was late. By ten thirty she decided Theresa must be dead, because she always arrived at the office before anyone else.

She had her hand on the phone to try to find out what had happened when she heard voices in the lobby outside her office.

She tucked a stray curl behind her ear as Baxter Dempsey stuck his prematurely receding hairline through the door.

"Hey, Cassie," he said, despite her having given him many broad hints that she hated the nickname. "Bet you've noticed that Theresa isn't here." Already, Cass didn't like the way the conversation was heading. "She had a family emergency. Nothing serious," Baxter continued before she could interrupt. "But she doesn't know how long she'll be off work. Could be a few weeks."

A surprising twinge of hurt plucked at Cass. Theresa had called someone else in the company rather than her? What was up with that? She knew she hadn't made many friends in the five months she'd been in this department, but she'd thought Theresa, at least, had warmed up to her.

"So we've found you a temporary assistant," Baxter finished, and she looked past him into a pair of very direct, wet-dream-inducing, laser-blue eyes.

The world faded slightly as the blood rushed from her head to her vital organs. What was the saying?

What happens in Vegas stays in Vegas.

The conference had been in Ottawa, not Vegas, but she'd hoped the same rules applied. She'd never expected the bartender she'd spent the night with two years ago to show up in her Halifax office.

As her new administrative assistant.

He's Olivia's father.

Hot faded to cold. Oh God. How much worse could this day get?

"Are you okay, Cassie?" Baxter stepped into her space. "It's nothing to get all worked up about. I'm sure everything will be fine and Theresa will be back soon. Until then, I want you to meet Logan Alexander. Logan, this is Cassiopeia Stone."

Cass held her breath, fully expecting Logan to indicate in some way that they'd already met.

Instead, without a hint of recognition, he approached her desk and extended a hand to her. "It's a pleasure, Ms. Stone. I hope you don't mind me filling in on short notice like this."

How on earth had he gone from a bartender in a hotel in Ottawa to an admin assistant at Kramer Aerospace?

She couldn't figure out the critical path for that one, and she couldn't very well ask for an explanation. She rose to her feet, feeling as if she'd stepped into some alternate universe where up was down, and found her voice. "N-n-not at all."

His hand was cool, firm, slightly rough-palmed, and much as she remembered. In fact, she remembered far too much about that night. She would have expected time and the mojitos she'd inhaled to have clouded at least a bit of it.

On the other hand, what did it say about her that he didn't seem to remember any of it at all?

What did it say about him?

He was as tall as she remembered, and she knew all too intimately that the leanness under the dress shirt and casual trousers he wore was 99 percent solid muscle. His untidy, espresso-brown hair still had a tendency to flop forward above one eye. His sharp-angled face was as handsome as ever, yet he somehow managed to seem as if he could blend into a crowd anywhere and no one would give him a second glance.

Unless they looked into his eyes. They could be cool and direct and unreadable, as they were now, or filled with a bone-melting heat. She tried not to think about the hotness. It still did weird things to her knees, and this was so not the time or the place.

"Cassiopeia," he said. "That's an unusual name."

She hated it. According to her mother, when she'd mentioned how pretty Cass was as a newborn, her father had decided to name her after a vain queen in Greek mythology. She'd never been sure who the underlying message was meant for, her mother or her. "My father's an unusual man."

She stepped around her desk and smiled for Baxter, who was watching her in a way she didn't particularly like. She wondered if this was some sort of test because he didn't think she could work with a male admin assistant.

It wasn't as if she was doing so great with the other men in the office, so perhaps his opinion was justified.

"Why don't I show Logan where we keep the office supplies and get the IT department to hook him up with a password for Theresa's computer?" She turned to Logan. "I assume you're familiar with the various office software programs and electronic filing systems?"

"Yes, Ma'am."

Yes, Ma'am. Mortification tightened her cheeks at the tiny, echoing reminder of her attempt at a role-playing game. She'd tried to be the dominatrix and he'd humored her.

Best night of her life.

His bland, friendly expression gave nothing away. If he'd been trying to get a rise out of her, she couldn't tell.

Since he didn't seem to recognize her—and she should be thankful for that, not insulted—she wasn't about to do or say anything that might remind him.

She remembered the photo of Olivia she had on her desk and tried not to panic. As soon as she could, she'd put it in a drawer out of sight. He might not put two and two together if he saw it, but she wasn't taking that chance.

How ironic that only this morning she'd been thinking it might be time to find Olivia a father. But this one was as unsuitable as it was possible for her to imagine.

He'd been fun. She'd grant him that.

But two years later, he still hadn't found any direction in life. Logan Alexander had *irresponsible* written all over him.

Chapter Three

Logan tried to decide how he felt that the elusive Mary Smith, who'd filled most of his late-night fantasies for the past two years, turned out to be an acting director in the company he was currently investigating.

He'd recognized her from her security photo the instant he'd seen it, which had bumped the personnel file he'd gotten from Dempsey to the top of his to-be-read pile. Then he'd discovered she'd been off on maternity leave and started ticking off the months on sweaty fingers before common sense finally kicked in.

She'd taken precautions. There was no way Miss Mary, who'd been so careful that they not be seen together, would have gotten pregnant by accident. Not by a bartender for sure. She was far too ambitious for that. He'd known it then and he could see it now in the way she kept glancing from him to Dempsey, worried Logan might give her away.

But his heart was still pounding from shock, and there

was this little, niggling doubt in the back of his head that said he might want to check this out, just to be sure.

He was nowhere near ready to be anyone's daddy. Not at this point in his life. He didn't even have his own home. He stored his belongings in a room at his sister's. His two nephews were all he could handle.

He listened carefully as Cass showed him around the office, introducing him to the staff. As she did, he paid particular attention to the office dynamics. These guys were divided into two camps. They either didn't like her or didn't take her seriously. None of them expected her to be their director for long, so they didn't bother offering her any more than a surface respect.

They didn't like the idea of a male admin assistant any more than they did a woman boss. Logan could feel the love in the air. He wasn't oblivious to the smirks either. Baxter Dempsey had himself a good sense of humor by offering him this position.

It had only taken Logan two seconds to realize that Dempsey, who sported a wide gold wedding band, had the hots for Cassiopeia Stone, whose fingers were bare. Logan couldn't blame him because he found her irresistible himself, but Mrs. Dempsey might not be quite as understanding.

Cass was as pretty as he remembered. He'd instantly loved all that curly, sun-streaked hair two shades short of brown, the wide hazel eyes sparkling with life, and the faint dusting of freckles on her nose. She'd looked like such an innocent when she walked into the bar with that lieutenant colonel.

A few hours after that, she'd proved looks could be deceiving.

She still couldn't lie worth a damn, though. That cute little stutter was a major nervous tell. And her whole body went stiff whenever she caught his eye, as if she'd have to bend at the waist to get a good look at her shoes. He wondered how long she was going to pretend she didn't recognize him.

Perhaps it was best if they left it at that. As much as he'd like to reacquaint himself with her, he had a job to do.

And Cass, unfortunately, was currently in his crosshairs.

While he supposed anything was possible, he didn't really believe she was the leak. She'd have to be a far better liar than this. He'd have to mention to his superiors that he knew her, however. If not, his investigation could be worth squat. He couldn't take an espionage case into a courtroom with even the slightest hint of a conflict of interest attached to it. The prosecution would eat him alive.

The workstation she showed him to was across from her office door and conveniently next to the classified publications closet, so all in all, he felt the position Dempsey had found for him within the company was a good one. Whether Dempsey had intended for it to be was another matter.

Logan settled himself at the computer and spent the remainder of the morning surfing through Theresa's files, trying to decide how deep he could dig without IT questioning what he was up to.

Pretty far, as it turned out. Admin assistants had a lot of access, and if ever asked what he was doing, he could chalk his nosiness up to trying to familiarize himself with the scope of the job.

The actual personnel performance files for Cass's staff were in her office under lock and key. He'd try and have a look at them after she left for the day.

Hello. What was this?

He opened a file marked "Birthdays" and Cass's name appeared at the top with a red flag beside it. Well, well. Miss Mary was twenty-seven today. He would never have guessed, and he was pretty good at things like that.

He glanced in her office. Her head was down and she was focused on some paperwork, chewing on the inside of her lip. She tapped her pen against her forehead, then scrawled some words across the top of a report. She'd draped her suit jacket over the back of her chair. The collar of her blouse was unbuttoned. And Logan envisioned another game they could play.

Man, she was sexy. She'd worn that same intent look on her face as she'd straddled him in bed, giving him all kinds of fun orders he'd been more than willing to obey.

But she was too girlie for such a male-dominated office. Someone should tell her to forego the fancy manicures and expensive power suits. They might be okay for her boardroom meetings, but not down here in the trenches where everyone else dressed office casual.

He went over and knocked on her door. "Ms. Stone? Mind if I take my lunch break?"

She looked up, distracted, then her forehead smoothed. Wariness crept into her eyes, deepening their rich hazel color. "Go ahead."

She ate her own lunch at her desk.

He didn't blame her. He doubted if she'd be any more welcome in the lunchroom than he was, although the difference was, he didn't care if he was welcome or not. He had a job to do, and right now, it involved a little male

bonding.

He got his sandwich from the fridge. Then, he sat at a table across from two geriatric, retired military men carrying on a heated debate over popular conspiracy theories and the probability of alien abductions.

It was nice to know the fate of their country had once been in such capable hands.

All in all, in the end, lunch was a bust. He didn't learn a thing that he couldn't have learned by watching one of those pseudo-documentary shows on cable.

He wandered back to his desk. Cass still sat at hers.

A tall man, broad-chested, midthirties, and carrying a Styrofoam lunch tray in one hand and a can of cola in the other, stepped off the elevator.

Inside, Logan sighed. He knew the type. This one wouldn't be able to resist the new office entertainment.

He hiked his can of cola in Logan's direction. "Hey, New Guy. You need any help carrying those files around, you let me know. Wouldn't want you breaking a nail or anything."

"Back atcha," Logan said. "You need help figuring out how to get back to your computer, I'll draw you a map." From the corner of his eye, he saw Cass's head come up from the papers she'd been frowning over.

The other guy stopped in his tracks and did a double take. Then he laughed, changed direction, and crossed the foyer to the front desk. He set the drink on the counter and reached over to offer Logan his hand.

"Jason," he said as they shook.

"Logan."

"So, Logan." Jason eyed him up and down. "Interesting career choice. Not one I'd have expected."

"It's a calling." Logan tipped back and locked his fingers behind his neck. "Actually, I happened to be in the right place at the right time. I'd just signed on at a temp agency because I needed some fast cash for airfare, and they called me last night. Once I'm done here, I'm off to tend bar in the sunny Caribbean. *Despedida.*" *Good-bye.*

"Congratulations," Jason said. "I hear it's hard to get work visas for some of those countries."

He stretched his eyes wide. "The Caribbean isn't a country?"

Jason drummed his fingers on the counter a few beats, then picked up his drink. "Good luck with that plan." He cracked open the can of cola and took a sip from it as he walked away, shaking his head.

Sometimes, his job could be fun.

Cass had heard the entire exchange. When he checked to see her reaction, she bent her head so fast that he couldn't catch a good look at her face.

And other times, not so much.

But she'd known him as a bartender and he had to give her a good reason as to why he was here. She was smart. She'd connect the dots. If it did turn out she was guilty, it wouldn't take her long to question why he'd also been working in a bar at a hotel where a Department of National Defence conference was taking place.

The rest of the afternoon dragged. There wasn't much he could do with Cass watching him, and although she tried not to be obvious about it, she watched him frequently. She twirled a stray curl around a finger as she worked, her pretty face rapt with concentration as she read through some files. Then he'd make some move or a deliberate loud noise, and her attention would shift to the reception area.

And him.

No, he doubted very much if she was the leak. He didn't think that was personal bias speaking either. She was way too jumpy for espionage.

Memories, warm and intense, flooded his thoughts, taking him back in time. He'd loved the feel of those curls brushing against his bare skin. She was ticklish too, but only on the bottom of her right foot.

Of all the things he'd had to do in his life, the one thing he regretted most was slipping out of her hotel room while she pretended to sleep in order to help her avoid the awkwardness he knew would come in the morning.

He wondered what the father of her baby was like. Logan couldn't imagine him slipping away after a night spent with Cass.

Under different circumstances he wouldn't have, either.

...

Cass sat on her sofa and scrolled through the website on her tablet with her thumb. *It's a legitimate dating service*, her friend Patricia had insisted. *I met John through it.*

Cass had to admit they seemed happily married.

She'd met Patricia through the daycare and liked her a lot. Patricia had always been friendly without being too nosy or judgmental, not like some of the others, and had invited her to ladies' wine night at her house a few times. She was one of the rare people Cass actually trusted.

It wasn't easy to meet suitable men, Patricia reminded her. The bar scene was totally out. Since Cass couldn't afford a singles cruise, or take Olivia along on one if she could, she'd have to resort to the dating service instead.

She wasn't sure she was comfortable with this. She didn't like leaving decisions to chance. She was going to ask a few questions before she filled out any profile online. It wasn't that she didn't trust Patricia's judgment. It was the possibility that Patricia and John's happy marriage was an outlier.

The baby monitor beside her crackled with static. She heard Olivia sigh in her sleep, and the rustle of blankets as she rolled around in her crib.

Deepening twilight streamed through her living room windows. She'd been given an exceptionally good deal on the purchase of the house because the previous owner had been forced into a nursing home, but all of its contents had been stripped, leaving it bare and forlorn-looking and showing its years of neglect. She'd decided to renovate one room at a time. The kitchen had been first, this room second, and she loved them both.

Her work laptop sat on the antique escritoire she'd picked up at an estate sale. Heavy leather furniture, dark brown, filled the room. She'd painted the walls creamy beige, and floral curtains puddled on the hardwood floor at either side of narrow, floor-to-ceiling windows. Scattered vases of flowers on small occasional tables gave the room a feminine feel.

The formal dining room was next on her list. She planned to turn that into a playroom for Olivia. The six bedrooms, and future home theater and family room, were all going to have to wait.

She plopped the tablet on the coffee table, tucked her bare feet beneath her, and rested her cheek against an ornamental sofa cushion.

Suitable men might be hard to find, but unsuitable ones cropped up everywhere and in the worst places. She'd had a hard time concentrating all day, knowing one of them was sitting at the workstation right outside her office. She hoped Theresa got her family emergency straightened out soon. Then Logan could go away and she could stop feeling so—

She should just get this over with.

Wiping her palms on the legs of her shorts, she punched in the number she found.

"Discreet Dating Service," chirped a cheery voice.

The kitchen doorbell sounded.

Heart pounding, Cass hit the off button on her phone without saying a word. She swung her feet to the floor, glad for the interruption. She really needed to work up more nerve before she made that call.

She opened the kitchen door. Mrs. Sheridan stood on her back deck, holding a cake.

"Surprise!" she said, thrusting the cake into Cass's suddenly numb hands.

The real surprise was standing at Mrs. Sheridan's back with an equally startled look on his face that he wiped away so quickly, Cass thought she might have been mistaken.

"Thank you," she managed to choke out, steadying the plate so the cake didn't slide to the floor. "How did you know it's my birthday?" She shot Logan a sharp look.

He shrugged, palms up, wordlessly telling her he didn't have any idea either.

"You told me when you moved in," Mrs. Sheridan said, all bright-eyed and unaware that Cass wanted nothing more than to slam the door and shoot the dead bolt on the pair of them. "The house was your birthday present to you and Olivia last year, wasn't it?"

She was touched that Mrs. Sheridan had remembered it.

She was less touched to have Logan standing on her doorstep, about to be invited into her kitchen, because as much as she'd like to, she couldn't very well ask his grandmother in but tell him to go away.

She hadn't bothered picking up the plush toys and building blocks scattered around the kitchen floor, and that, too, made her nervous. She saved housework for weekends.

Her cheeks warmed with guilt. She'd tried to get in touch with him when she'd found out she was pregnant, she reminded herself. Now it was too late. She no longer felt like sharing Olivia. The thought of him demanding custody or visitation rights made her heart beat a little faster, even though she knew the prospect was unlikely.

She also knew he'd been jerking Jason around when he said he thought the Caribbean was a country, but she didn't doubt for a second that he was soon headed to one of the islands. A bar-tending gig on a beach was right up his alley. She'd have to find out which one so she could avoid it in the future.

"This is my grandson, Logan. Logan, meet Cass Stone," Mrs. Sheridan said.

He smiled at Cass in a way she couldn't begin to interpret. All she knew was that it lit fires in places she'd almost forgotten.

She prayed for someone to put her out of her misery. Not only had she spent a night having wild sex with her new admin assistant, it turned out she'd slept with her sweet, elderly neighbor's grandson, too.

The whole world was against her today.

"We've already met," he said, and her stomach tried to crawl out of her body through her toes. "She's my new boss."

She didn't hear any innuendo in his tone and breathed a little easier. That was the one good thing in all this. He couldn't possibly remember her, because if he did, there was no way he could refer to her as his boss in front of his grandmother. Not after their role-playing game.

"Where's Olivia?" Mrs. Sheridan asked. Her face fell. "Is she in bed already?"

"She's been falling asleep around seven. Daycare tuckers her out." At least that much had gone right.

"What a shame." Mrs. Sheridan turned to her grandson. "You should see Olivia. She looks like your sister did at that age, except for the curls."

He froze. Cass forgot how to breathe.

Because Olivia also looked like Logan.

He raised an eyebrow at his grandmother. The corner of his mouth quivered with humor. "Let me guess. She's got brown hair and blue eyes. Admit it, Nan. Babies all look alike."

"Let's cut the c-c-cake," Cass said.

She got out plates and napkins while Mrs. Sheridan chatted happily away, filling the kettle for a pot of tea. She knew her way around Cass's kitchen quite well. She often stopped over for a chat in the evenings and to play with Olivia.

Logan was looking around with open interest. The kitchen gleamed with state-of-the-art, stainless-steel appliances and granite countertops. He let out a low whistle from between his teeth. "Nice."

Cass wasn't entirely sure he meant that as a compliment. If he was jealous of other people's lifestyles, he should work a little harder to improve his own. She looked at him sharply, but he met her gaze with polite innocence.

Again, she felt that odd, disturbing little wobble in her knees when she looked into his eyes. They didn't reflect a man with very little ambition. The intelligence she saw hinted he had far more to him than he let on to the world. That was what had attracted her to him in the first place.

And he'd taken to the administrative position as if he'd been doing it for years. He'd be bored to death inside of a week.

"Logan's handy. He could take a look at your car for you if you'd like," Mrs. Sheridan offered, reaching for a tin filled with tea bags.

"Always happy to check under a hood," he added.

Cass eyed him with wary suspicion. He smiled back at her, the picture of innocence.

"Thank you, that's v-v-very nice, but it's under warranty. The dealer already picked it up," she replied.

"If you're going to be without a car for a while, then Logan could always drive you to work. I told him he could use mine as much as he likes."

He leaned back in a kitchen chair, stretching his long, denim-clad legs out in front of him, and watched her reaction with undisguised interest. He all but dared her to refuse the offer, and that ticked her off. He acted as if she thought she was too good to fraternize with her staff.

She was no snob. She'd worked her way up in the world. Nothing had been handed to her.

But she didn't think she could drive back and forth to

work with a man she'd played sex games with. Even if he had no recollection of them, she did. In vivid detail.

And she had a daughter as proof.

Oh God.

He decided to take pity on her, which only annoyed her more.

"I'll be riding my bike, Nan. Ms. Stone isn't going to want to travel to work on that."

This, too, was what had initially attracted her to him. He'd been kind and considerate. So what was wrong with her that she couldn't accept the out he offered her now?

Partly because she was no coward. And maybe because it freaked her out more than a little to hear that smooth voice calling her "Ms. Stone" instead of "Ms. Smith."

"My name is Cass. And you won't want to ride your bike in the rain, will you?" she pointed out to him. "You're welcome to drive with me on those days."

Mrs. Sheridan unplugged the whistling kettle. "You know I don't like you riding that motorcycle, Logan. If you won't use my car, once Cass gets hers back, you can drive to work with her. There's no sense in taking two vehicles when you're both going to the same place."

And that, Cass told herself, was what had always gotten her in trouble in the past. It seemed she still hadn't grasped the difference between daring and downright stupidity.

Chapter Four

His grandmother's comment about Cass's daughter had thrown Logan off. Worse, it had unsettled Cass, too.

He tamped down emotions he wasn't ready to touch. He dealt in facts that would need to stand up in court. Gut instincts alone weren't enough. He wasn't jumping to any conclusions. Not without proof.

Unfortunately, now he was going to have to become more objective about Cass, because she had some seriously expensive tastes. He had no idea how she'd managed to acquire a house in his grandmother's rather exclusive, if somewhat rundown, suburban neighborhood.

Given the easy commute into the city, and how close it was to the ocean, this was a prime piece of real estate. The people who lived in Cornwall might not be wealthy, but most came from what was known as old money. Their properties tended to be inherited.

Cass's security clearance said she had no family. A little

digging had already told him they were estranged, and he guessed it was irreconcilable because that was the only way she could have gotten around the requirement to account for them on the forms.

Her juvenile records were off-limits, but if she'd ever gotten in trouble with the law, she'd turned her life around a long time ago. She'd worked her way through school with scholarships. She made a good salary. At his insistence, Dempsey had already filled him in on how much she earned.

But if the rest of the house looked like her kitchen…

Well, he'd have to find a way to check that out. If she wasn't independently wealthy, she had to be carrying a serious debt load.

Maybe the father of her baby was helping her out.

The same guy who'd left her sitting home alone on her birthday.

More emotions, most of them paralyzing, again tried to lead Logan in a direction he had no wish to go. He thrust them aside with a ruthlessness he hadn't known he possessed.

"What happened to Mrs. Calaveccio?" he asked, directing the question to his grandmother in reference to the previous homeowner, and the neighbor he'd assumed they were coming to visit. He hadn't seen her since he was about twelve, the last time he'd spent a summer with his grandmother, but he had fond memories of Mrs. Calaveccio's cookies. Chocolate chip. Moist and chewy.

It was funny how life got away from a person. His parents had moved the family to Toronto the year before that summer, and he'd been homesick, so he'd come to stay with his grandmother for a few months. After that he'd started making new friends in Toronto, gotten involved in sports and school activities, and suddenly, his grandmother had been the one who'd had to do the visiting. He'd stayed with her whenever he was passing through Nova Scotia on business, and always tried to get in a few quick home repairs when he did, but still, it had been five years since he'd seen her last.

He felt like the world's worst grandson.

"Mabel's in a nursing home," his grandmother replied, some of the sunshine fading from her bright eyes. "She was in the early stages of Alzheimer's, so when she was diagnosed, we all helped her settle her affairs. Dave Bishop's son is a judge. She gave him power of attorney and he sold the house for her." She reached over and patted Cass's hand. "Mabel wanted it to go to someone who'd love it, and we all knew by the look on Cass's face when she saw it that she planned to stay."

That was right. He remembered that Mrs. Calaveccio didn't have any family of her own. And because the people in this neighborhood had all known each other since the beginning of time, of course they'd step up to help her out.

Maybe Dave Bishop's son, the judge, was the baby's father. Logan dredged up the hazy image of a skinny, redheaded teen with big teeth, about three years older than he was. Logan couldn't picture him with Cass, but he also couldn't see him as a judge. Time did things to people.

"Cass usually takes some of us to visit her on the weekends," his grandmother was saying. "She bought a big new minivan and everything."

Well, well. He didn't know what to make of that.

"That's generous of you," he said to Cass.

Her face reddened. "There's a grocery store and a mall

two blocks away from the nursing home. While they're visiting with her, I run errands. It works out well for everyone."

He took a sip of the tea she set before him, then attacked the piece of cake on the Royal Doulton plate. He'd never known anyone to actually use showy china before. His mother and his grandmother kept theirs in fancy cabinets. Their everyday china was heavy and plain.

Cass was a study of contradictions. Fresh-faced, but willing to experiment sexually. High-powered, upwardly mobile, probably living well beyond her means, but a single mother who made the time to drive her elderly neighbors around on weekends. She wore pricey business attire at the office. Here at home she sat across from him in a T-shirt, blue jeans, fuzzy pink slippers and a curly ponytail, looking about as girl next door as she could be.

And sexy as hell.

Yeah. She could be selling military secrets. Or preying on the elderly. She could also be building Habitats for Humanity. Con men—or con women—didn't have the word CRIMINAL tattooed on their foreheads. Unease settled deeper in his stomach.

He couldn't believe she was that good a liar. Not with that stutter. And her smile. It stretched all the way to her eyes and made her look as if she were up to no good, but the kind of no good that could get a guy naked.

Not the kind that involved espionage.

Or lying to a baby's father, even if by omission.

"Mind if I use your bathroom?" he asked, scraping his chair against the inlaid tile floor as he pushed back from the table.

Cass showed him to the powder room off the front foyer. As she did, he took a good look into her living room, also off the foyer, and at the new, hand-carved oak stairwell leading to the second floor.

While he washed his hands in the small bathroom sink, he considered the situation. He wanted to think the best of her. He didn't want to find out he'd been so totally wrong.

And that was a problem.

When he came out of the bathroom she was busy in the kitchen talking to his grandmother, so he ducked into the living room. Snooping in someone's home wasn't really sanctioned, but this was becoming personal.

Her laptop sat on a small desk. Papers were strewn over her sofa and the floor in front of it. A tablet rested on the coffee table. It had a phone listing for a dating service on its open window.

He tapped redial on her phone and watched as a number popped up on display, then hung up before it could ring through. He compared the number against the listing on the tablet. And there it was.

Definitely no man in her life, at least not right now.

This had been a day crammed full of surprises.

He poked carefully through the spread of papers but found nothing unusual. He longed to take a closer look at her laptop, but didn't dare. There were privacy laws he had to follow, and he had no business being in her living room as it was.

Her office at work was another matter entirely. He'd been given permission by her company to search both it and its contents.

He left her laptop alone, but stared long and hard at the

tablet. She'd have baby pictures on it. He could hear Cass's and his grandmother's quiet voices, muffled by the closed kitchen door.

He reached out with one finger and tapped the screen. The background display was set with an image of a toddler in a pink mud suit, covered in dirt and sitting in an empty flower bed.

It was too hard to say who she looked like.

A cold lump of ice had formed in the pit of his stomach. Practicality said he should leave this alone until he'd finished his investigation. He didn't want to get his personal life tangled up with his work. A few more weeks wouldn't make any difference.

He'd been gone too long as it was, and they had to be wondering what he was up to. He tapped the screen again, putting it back as he'd found it.

He returned to the kitchen and reclaimed his seat at the table.

"I was checking out the finish work in your living room," he said. "It's all original?"

She gave him an odd look. "The woodwork in the house is beautiful as is. I didn't see any reason to change it when other parts of the house need bigger repairs. I got as far as the bathroom upstairs." A rueful laugh escaped her. "Old houses cost a lot more to maintain than I'd expected."

"My dear, I know what you mean," his grandmother said to her, all sympathy and understanding. "I had to replace most of the windows in mine two winters ago."

The look of horror on Cass's face would have been comical in other circumstances. Now, it made Logan's stomach hurt. He pushed his empty plate away and picked up a fresh cup of tea.

Before anything more could be said, another knock sounded at the kitchen door and more neighbors filed in, putting an end to question period.

The impromptu birthday party gave him an opportunity to see how Cass interacted with the rest of the neighborhood. By the end of the evening he was more confused than ever.

And bothered.

At the office he could almost ignore the memories of the night he'd spent with her. Here in her home, where she was relaxed and laughing, he could see all too well the woman who'd caught his attention in that bar two years before. The thought of those curls spread across a crisp white pillowcase and the corners of her hazel eyes crinkling in laughter as he ran his hands across her bare stomach, still ignited desire deep inside him.

Her baby's father would have to be some kind of dumbass to walk away from all that.

Or maybe he'd been another casual hookup, one who wanted no part of a baby. It was equally possible she'd gotten pregnant on purpose, and some poor, unsuspecting schmuck had provided a stud service he didn't know about.

Logan couldn't figure her out. He'd been arrogant enough to think her one night with him had been an impetuous act of serendipity, an opportunity she hadn't been able to ignore. That the stars had somehow aligned. He hated thinking he might have been mistaken. Or that he was the schmuck.

He had no idea how her interest in online dating factored in.

She'd brought out more of the gold-trimmed china to serve people cake on, which meant she couldn't put the mounting stack of dirty dishes in the dishwasher.

"I'll wash," he said when a few of the ladies made noises about staying to help Cass with the cleanup.

Her cheeks flushed, and she avoided looking at him. "There's no need. I can do them."

"Don't be silly, dear," his grandmother said to her, sliding Logan a telling wink that made him feel awkward as hell. "You two young people can get them done in half the time as us old women, and with far less breakage. Logan doesn't mind. It's getting late and you both have to work tomorrow."

Cass looked about ready to crawl out of her skin, but had to know as well as he did that it was impossible to argue with a bunch of matchmaking old ladies.

"Well, that was certainly subtle," he said after everyone had gone, trying to make a joke out of it. Her obvious nervousness around him made him nervous, too.

He grabbed the dish soap and squirted a healthy amount into the sink under a stream of hot water. She reached past him for a cup towel. A waft of her soft-scented shampoo lingered in the air, and he breathed it in deep. She smelled every bit as good as she looked.

And like he remembered.

Except Mary Smith didn't exist. He had to push everything personal aside and concentrate on his job. He wanted to know more about Cass Stone, acting director.

"So what got you involved with a company that sells its services to the military?" he asked, plunging his hands into the hot, soapy water.

"Civil engineering."

He'd seen the small steel ring on her pinkie finger that told the world she had taken her oath as a professional engineer. He'd read her files. "Isn't technical publications a bit of a side road?"

She shrugged her slim shoulders. "Perhaps for an engineer, but not for advancement within the company. Plus, I can validate a lot of the technical data going into the publications, which is an added service that the customer values."

That explained why she brought home so much extra work. Running the department wouldn't leave her much spare time for validating source data during the day. She was ambitious, but he'd known that about her already. And smart. That was the part that worried him most.

"Why an engineer?" he asked, curious as to what had possessed her to go into such a male-dominated field of study.

"Why an administrative assistant?" she countered, and he gave a soft laugh as he passed her a saucer.

"Maybe I don't like to be pigeonholed. Maybe I like being able to move on when the mood strikes me."

"Maybe you should think about your future."

Her tone held a hint of disapproval. He leaned one hip against the sink and turned to look fully at her. On the surface, she seemed so uptight and proper. And yet he knew how every inch of that smooth skin felt beneath the stroke of his fingertips. He knew where to touch her to make her laugh. He knew the way she breathed, and the soft little sounds she made when he moved inside her.

And those thoughts were driving him nuts.

"What do you have against admin assistants?" he asked. "It's honest work."

"I don't have anything against admin assistants. But I do

believe people should strive to achieve their full potential. Sooner or later we all have to grow up."

"It's a job, Cass. It pays the bills. Some people think there are more important things in life than being defined by what they do to earn a living."

She polished the cup in her hand with such diligence she was in danger of wearing off its delicate pattern. After a moment she seemed to realize what she was doing and set it on the counter.

"What's important to you then, if not your work?" she asked.

He handed her the last of the flatware to dry, deliberately brushing his soapy knuckles the length of her forearm before he tipped them into her palm. She had him there because his work really was important to him, and he really did define himself by it.

But he couldn't say that to her.

"Life," he said lightly. "It's meant to be lived. And enjoyed."

A frown crossed her face. "The best way to enjoy it is if you have the money to do so."

"I don't need a lot to enjoy life."

"Just enough to get to the Caribbean?" She slid the flatware into a drawer, piece by piece, with careful precision. "You had everything you ever wanted or needed while you were growing up, didn't you?"

It was an easy assumption and not far from the truth. After all, she lived next door to his grandmother, who clearly would never have let her family go without. But she was looking at him as if he were someone to be pitied, and he didn't like that.

He was the one who'd taken on this role, he reminded himself. She'd formed the opinion he'd planted. And now, she was trying to figure him out, too.

She was clever. He had to keep her unsettled so she'd stop asking questions. He knew what would put some distance between them.

He plucked the cup towel from her fingers, then slid one palm to the back of her head and the other to the small of her back. Surprise deepened the color of her eyes as he drew her tight against him.

He gave her two seconds to think about what his next move might be. Then he dipped his chin and met her lips with his.

He hadn't forgotten how good she'd tasted two years ago, but he hadn't anticipated how much better she'd taste now. He'd only wanted to see if he could still make her respond, despite her less than flattering opinion of him.

And she did.

Her fingers curled into the front of his shirt, pulling her to her toes to meet his greater height, her mouth moving willingly beneath his. A soft sigh sounded low in her throat, and before he knew what was happening, his own fingers had slid beneath the thin fabric of her T-shirt to touch her bare skin.

Satisfaction filled him. No, she hadn't forgotten him, and no, he hadn't been mistaken about their one brief night together. The attraction was still there and most definitely mutual. Right now, if he wanted to, he could take this kiss to a whole other level.

But their present situation was far too complicated for that. His goal was to push her away. They already skated a fine line between personal and professional that could only cause problems neither one of them needed.

He caught her hands as they drifted to the waistband of his jeans and he held them, trying to breathe. "You're my boss at the office. It might be a bad idea for you to be my boss after hours, too." He couldn't resist. "Granted, I do enjoy taking orders from you."

Alarm deepened the hazel of her eyes. "I have no idea what you're talking about."

She still planned to pretend they were strangers. He ran his thumb across the soft pad of her wrist. "You aren't worried about what sleeping with your admin assistant might do to your career?"

Her mouth opened and closed.

"One of us should be thinking about consequences." He dropped her hands and took a step toward the door, then stopped with his own hand on the doorknob. "Happy birthday, Miss M-M-Mary. See you in the morning."

She touched her lips with trembling fingers and reached for the countertop behind her to steady herself. Her voice, although low, carried plainly as he shut the door behind him.

"I liked you better as a bartender," she'd whispered.

Chapter Five

Cass had thought about nothing but consequences, and Logan, all night.

Now Olivia wasn't cooperating, and Cass was tired and running behind. She wrestled her wriggling and protesting daughter into her jacket and pink rubber boots, then plopped her, kicking and screaming, into her stroller.

Spring had arrived, and the morning smelled of damp earth and freshness, but the air remained cool. Cass grabbed her own jacket off a hook in the narrow front entry and locked the door behind her. She'd chosen more sensible shoes so she could race for the bus if she had to. The dealer had offered her the use of a car, but sworn her own would be ready that afternoon and they'd drop it off at her office, so she'd turned it down.

One of Olivia's boots came off, and Cass bent down to reclaim it. She stroked a finger down her daughter's plump, soft-skinned cheek and met her stormy, tear-glazed blue eyes as she slipped the boot back on her tiny foot.

"Love you oodles, Livs," she said, and just like that, the tantrum was over. Olivia smiled at her, blinking tears off her long lashes, and Cass's heart melted.

"Cute kid. Great set of lungs, too."

Startled, Cass almost toppled on her backside. She dropped a hand to the asphalted driveway to steady herself. When she looked behind her, Logan stood a few feet away. He wore a thigh-hugging pair of gray dress pants and a dark sports jacket over a white turtleneck sweater. The jacket fit him well across the shoulders. The dress pants, even better. His expression as he stared down at her and Olivia was completely unreadable.

It hadn't been at all unreadable last night when he'd kissed her.

Happy birthday, Miss M-M-Mary.

He remembered her. No question about that. But he was different from the man she recalled. Harder. This time, she didn't feel safe around him.

Not at all.

"What are you doing here?" she asked, standing. She smoothed her hand down her skirt and positioned herself between him and Olivia, although she suspected the damage had already been done. The math wasn't difficult. He'd recognize his own eyes, too.

But only if he wanted to, and she didn't believe that he did. He was older than she was, likely around thirty, yet he possessed no career aspirations whatsoever. His current employment was low income and temporary, just as it was when she'd first met him. He was all about enjoying life. He'd said it himself.

She'd been all about fun and adventure once, too. But she'd had to grow up. Logan wasn't quite there yet, and maybe never would be.

He jingled the keys in his palm up and down a few times. "Nan insisted I take her car and offer you a ride to work."

Her lips tugged at the corners. His enthusiasm seemed about equal to hers, making the whole situation so awkward it was either laugh or run screaming. "That was gracious of her."

He didn't smile. Neither did he apologize for his wording or try to repair it. He simply stood there, watching her, until the silence grew too long for comfort.

She hunched deeper into her jacket, bracing against a gust of damp wind that rattled the naked tree limbs. Olivia arched her back and tried to crawl out of the stroller, and Cass placed a hand on the knitted cap covering her baby-fine curls to keep her from wriggling out of the safety harness.

"I have to take my daughter to daycare, and I don't want to hold you up," she said. "I'll catch the bus."

"My boss will understand if I'm a few minutes late." He finally smiled a little, but it held zero warmth. "I doubt very much if tardiness will be an issue for her."

Some instinct inside her, some sense of self-preservation that had served her well in the past, warned her not to argue with him right now. This wasn't Logan the admin assistant or the good-natured bartender or the fun hookup who'd played sex games with her that she faced.

This Logan was angry.

The very real possibility that he might actually want Olivia shook Cass. She had once been the ultimate in risk takers. Not anymore. Not with her daughter.

An overwhelming possessiveness caught her off guard. Olivia was *hers*.

Right then and there, she decided she'd deny it if he asked. She'd already put *Father Unknown* on the birth certificate.

"I'll be back in about twenty minutes," she said, afraid he'd offer to walk with them, too.

He didn't. He simply stood and watched her until they rounded the corner.

Ten minutes later, as she was leaving Olivia at daycare, she bumped into her friend Patricia coming in. Her BMW was parked at the curb in front of the building, the engine running.

"There's a hottie sitting on your front steps," Patricia said. Curiosity gleamed in her eyes, but she didn't ask any questions.

"That's my neighbor's grandson," Cass replied. "He's giving me a ride to work because my car's in the garage."

Patricia's eyebrows went up as she kissed the top of her little boy's blond head and scooted him off to the playroom with the palm of her hand. "I could use a ride like that, although believe me, I wouldn't be taking it to work."

She was too flustered to respond with more than a mumble. She didn't dare stop to chat for long. Logan wouldn't head for the office without her. If she thought he would, she'd ring for a cab from the daycare. If she did that, however, she'd bet when she came home after work he'd be waiting for her.

"I'll call you tonight," Patricia said. "If you aren't interested in the hottie, then I have someone I'd like you to meet."

She nodded, not really listening. She took one last look at Olivia before leaving the daycare, then scurried up the sunny sidewalk toward home as fast as she could. As she approached her street corner, she forced herself to slow down. She'd hitchhiked to Montreal at the age of fifteen to see her favorite band in concert. Facing Logan was nothing compared to that.

He sat on her front steps, staring at his hands clasped between his bent knees. His dark hair was cut shorter than it had been in Ottawa and spiked up in places as if he'd run his fingers through it. He lifted his head when he heard her footsteps. Faint black stubble shadowed his jaw, indicating he was a bedtime shaver, not a morning man. She remembered the feel of that stubble.

Against her throat. Her breasts. The inside of her thighs.

Those laser-like blue eyes zeroed in on her face and she lost her breath. Patricia was right. Definitely a hottie. Cass remembered that, too. And after that kiss in her kitchen last night, she couldn't deny she still responded to him.

But he wasn't the man she wanted in Olivia's life, or in her own. So far the only things to recommend him were that he was great in bed, had a basic sense of decency—if not priorities—and a nice grandmother.

Who subsidized his living expenses.

She didn't want a man she had to look after any more than she wanted one looking after her. She wanted a partner.

More than anything, she wanted Olivia off-limits to Logan.

She was signing up for that dating service as soon as she got home from work.

Pain—hot, breathtaking, and unexpected—burrowed a wormhole deep into Logan's heart. All of the feelings he'd tried to ignore bubbled up. One look at Olivia and he'd seen his younger sister's face, and there was no doubt in his mind who her father was.

He was the schmuck.

It turned out that suspecting was one thing, and knowing for certain, another. He'd been totally blindsided by the intensity of his feelings the second he'd seen his daughter's face. Two days ago, he'd have sworn a child was the last thing he wanted.

Now, she was all he could think of.

Cass had stolen two years of her development and life from him that he'd never get back, and that was going to be hard to forgive. She could have found him if she'd tried hard enough.

If she'd tried at all. She'd made it quite plain that he didn't impress her. That he didn't measure up to her standards. That he wasn't good enough for more than scratching an itch.

Those were all things he'd made certain she thought, so he wasn't blameless in this, but it still took him the entire twenty-six minutes she was gone to admit that hating her was the wrong reaction.

He'd come to a decision during those painful twenty-six minutes of waiting on her steps for her to return. The ethical thing to do would be to remove himself from this assignment. He couldn't do that. He was human. It would make it too hard to get this close to his daughter again because even if he removed himself, he still wouldn't be able to tell Cass why he was here.

He'd have to suck this up and carry on with his current role, but it meant he couldn't confront her about Olivia. The second he did, he'd be in a conflict of interest, and Logan wanted to find out who was selling government secrets more than he needed to press her on a truth he already knew. He owed it to the memory of his brother-in-law, and to his sister and nephews, to do his job and do it right.

He'd see this case through to the end, and he'd compromise nothing. Then, when it was over, he and Cass were going to talk. She might not be guilty of stealing classified government information, but he knew for a fact that she'd stolen two years and a daughter from him. Until he was done this assignment, she was going to see far more of him than she liked.

His chest pounded with longing, suppressed hurt, and anger. One way or another, he intended to get to know his daughter. He already knew she was beautiful. And he loved the name Olivia. He wished with all his heart that he'd had input into the decision.

He abandoned the front steps to join Cass as she walked up the driveway toward him.

"Ready?" he asked, gripping the car keys tight in his fist as he struggled for calm.

She nodded.

He let her lead the way through the break in the hedge, then got behind the wheel of his grandmother's convertible, a 1976 Triumph TR6 in a British racing green that she rarely drove anymore. He'd tried to buy it off her a few times, but it had belonged to his grandfather and she refused to part with it, even though she never minded Logan driving it. He'd been taking it out since he was sixteen years old.

"This is safer than a motorcycle?" she asked as she fumbled for the seat belt.

He reached across her to snag it from between the seat back and the car door. His cheek pressed into her shoulder, her mass of curly hair tickling his nose, his own shoulder rubbing across her breasts as he moved. She smelled like she'd been handling a baby, all fresh and new and clean, and he had to close his eyes for a second and fight hard to catch his breath. She pressed into the bucket seat, whether to give him more room or to avoid him touching her, he couldn't be sure. He clicked the seat-belt prong into the receiver clip near the transmission mount and straightened, trying not to stare at her long, sheer-nylon-clad legs, but he couldn't bring himself to look at her face. This odd combination of anger and desire he was feeling toward her threw him off balance. He didn't want to want her.

What he wanted was his daughter.

He had so many questions about Olivia that he didn't dare ask. Not yet. The shock was too fresh, and he couldn't begin to pretend to be casual.

"What do you know about a TR6?" he asked instead as he started the car and backed out of the driveway.

She spouted off stats that would have amazed him if he hadn't already known she was smart and an engineer. He slid a sidelong look in her direction, immediately wishing he hadn't.

She knew he knew about Olivia. Her hazel eyes were fixed on him, bright and filled with a caution that told him she was as afraid as he was of his reaction to the discovery he was the father.

She should be. She had lied by omission and stolen his daughter from him, and it was hard for him to remember she was also a mother who believed she was protecting her child.

From an evil administrative assistant and former bartender.

Anger, and worse, impotent frustration, burned at the backs of his eyes. Money did not make the man. He had files full of proof that it quite often did the exact opposite. There was nothing more important than being a decent human being. Nothing. That was the value he wanted his daughter to learn.

There was also a tiny chance — a very slight one — that he wanted his daughter to be proud of him for more than that.

"I'm better with the components of military aircraft," Cass was saying.

He turned onto the main street and into morning rush-hour traffic and struggled to remember what they'd been talking about.

Convertibles. He should be thinking about work instead, and this was a good opportunity to pick her brain.

"Tell me a little about the men in the office," he said. "Are they all retired military?" He slowed the car for a corner. "And are they all such chauvinists?"

"Two of the writers are women." She fiddled with the handle on her laptop bag, now tucked between their seats like a barrier. "They aren't all retired military, but Kramer Aerospace builds on its customer relations by hiring qualified candidates from within military families as much as possible. The translators are wives who work from home."

He already knew all the details of every member of her staff. It was the retired military who interested him most.

"Do the women dislike you, too?" He got a perverse sort of pleasure from pointing out her lack of popularity in the department. Too much, really, but he couldn't seem to help it.

"It's not that any of them dislike me personally," she replied. "They think I'm too young and that I haven't earned this promotion. I didn't start at the bottom and work my way up, which is what they're used to. They think management is pushing me through the system to make me someone else's problem."

That, he knew, was the perception within the military. When bureaucrats had a problem with an officer's performance, they promoted him—or her—and moved them to a different department. Problem solved. As a manager and director, Cass was seen as an officer.

She had a backbone of steel and an impeccable track record with management. He didn't believe anyone was trying to unload her. She was a survivor.

"So what's their issue with me?" he asked.

All her attention was on him as she considered her answer. He'd liked that about her, the way she concentrated so hard on an activity. Back then, it helped that he'd liked what they were doing. He pushed those memories away. All he wanted from her now was information.

And access to his daughter.

"I don't think they've ever seen so much...*man*...doing what they consider a woman's job before. They can't figure you out and they don't like it."

Her assessment went a little deeper than his. If hers was

correct, and he thought it was, then he was willing to bet that a few of them, at least the ones into conspiracy theories, would soon start to wonder if Logan was CSIS. They knew how the military worked. It was part of his job to make sure he didn't raise any suspicions.

Lazy, lacking in ambition, and *head-in-the-clouds. Someone who'd never had to work for a living* was the image he had to continue to go for. *Someone who thought the Caribbean was a country.* Cass was already there in her opinion of him. He shifted gears a little too fast and the car lurched as a red light changed to green.

Those were the characteristics every woman wanted to find in the father of her child.

. . .

Cass stared through the car window. A foolish part of her was disappointed that she'd worried for nothing, because Logan showed not even a polite interest in Olivia. *Cute kid* and *great set of lungs* were the best he could do.

She'd wondered before, many times, why men didn't have the same attachment to their children that women did. Her father had never cared about her other than how she reflected on him. Her mother had cared, Cass didn't doubt that, but she did whatever she was told to do because she'd never been a strong person.

Maybe Cass was being too hard on Logan. She should be relieved, not disappointed, by his lack of interest in Olivia. She'd been the one who'd approached him in the bar. Neither one of them had anticipated the consequences.

She was strong enough to deal with them on her own.

She loved Olivia with all her heart, more than anything or anyone in the world, and didn't regret a thing.

They got to the office with minutes to spare.

She left him at the security desk filling out the necessary paperwork for parking his grandmother's car on company property.

She paused in the act of pressing the ancient elevator-call button, her finger hovering over the black plastic circle. Mrs. Sheridan, that sweet little old lady, was Olivia's great grandmother.

Guilt, hot and unexpected, swept over her, leaving her dizzy and with a tightening knot in her stomach. Mrs. Sheridan was already thrilled to be a part of Olivia's life. For the first time it occurred to Cass that, while Logan didn't seem to care about having a daughter, Olivia had other family who might. Cass was so used to relying on herself that she'd never considered the possibility. She tried to imagine explaining the situation to her neighbor. *Your grandson and I spent a hot night playing sex games. FYI, here's your great-granddaughter.*

That wasn't a conversation she could ever see herself having.

She punched the button. The doors groaned open, and she stepped inside. The elevator floor swayed beneath her feet. Seconds later, she stepped off at her floor and scrabbled in her jacket pocket for her office key.

It annoyed her to discover she didn't need it. The door had been left open again.

She dropped her laptop bag on a chair and booted up her computer. When she heard Logan at the front desk, she went out to speak to him.

"When you have time, could you call Maintenance and ask them to talk to the cleaners about locking the office doors behind them?" she asked. "This is the second time this week that I've come in to find mine open."

His head came up from the stack of papers he'd been sorting. His face went so still and intent that she felt an awkward urge to squirm. "Was anything touched?"

"They're cleaners," she said. "They touch everything."

"That's not what I meant."

"I know what you meant." She didn't like thinking it, either. "I keep the drawer with the petty cash locked and the key hidden."

"You have other things in your office. Like your computer."

"There are computers in all the cubicles."

"You have more access to efiles than anyone else in the department."

"Wrong. You do, and your computer is right out in the open," she pointed out. "Besides, without the password, logging in on mine is a waste of time."

Logan pushed past her and in a few long strides was inside her office and behind her desk, with her scurrying after him. He lifted the corner of her desk calendar and pulled out a scrap of paper with LIVVYBABY written on it.

He held it up. "You mean this password?"

"Have you been snooping through my desk?" She was outraged at the thought of him invading her privacy.

"Cass." He looked at her as if she were unbelievably dense. "It's in the same place I found Theresa's. I bet three quarters of the office have their password hidden under something on their desk or in a top drawer. Two of the writers scribbled theirs on sticky notes and stuck them on their computer monitors."

She hugged her elbows, hating to admit he was right. "Passwords have to be changed every three months. It's hard to remember them."

He settled into her chair, pulled it up to her desk, and jiggled her mouse. The gyrating screen flickered to life.

"What are you doing?" she asked.

"I'm pretty good with computers. I'm searching your history to see if anything confidential was accessed when you weren't in the office."

"This is ridiculous." She was torn between unease and exasperation, but unease was rapidly winning out and she didn't like to admit it. Despite the unlocked office door, this was a secure building. No one came in or out after hours without signing the log or without the proper security clearances. The premises were patrolled. "The commissionaire on rounds would notice if anyone was in my office. I have internet access in here. At the worst, it was someone looking up porn."

He glanced up from his task. "I find it interesting that porn was the first possibility you came up with. Been looking up spankings, have we? Has someone been a naughty girl?"

She couldn't let that pass by. "I'm more of a domme."

He chuckled softly. His voice dipped low, turning sexy and silky smooth. "Turnabout is fair play, Miss Mary. A little spanking might be just what you need. Ever consider letting someone else take charge for a change so you can see what you're missing?"

Heat pooled in her abdomen and left her legs shaky. When he called her *Miss Mary* and looked at her that way, all she could think of was how those blue eyes lit up during sex.

Right now they had a touch of ice to them, and her instincts screamed *danger*. He was trying to unsettle her. She wasn't sure he was entirely kidding about her needing a spanking either, and not in a good way. But that could simply be paranoia on her part.

She crooked loose curls behind one ear and moved behind him so she could see the monitor over his shoulder. "What makes you think I'm missing anything?"

"Between a baby and work, you've probably been too busy for *games*," he paused to let that word sink in, "for, what—I'm guessing twenty-four…twenty-five months?"

That sounded like a really long time. And yet, not long enough. She wondered if he was fishing, trying to find out if she'd been exclusive.

Maybe he was looking for proof that Olivia wasn't his.

"I don't kiss and tell," she said.

"Thank heavens. My reputation is safe." He went back to studying the monitor, his fingertips clicking away at the keys. After a few minutes he sat back, one hand resting on the keyboard, the other rubbing his chin as he frowned. "Everything's clean. No porn sites popped up, so all seems okay on that front. I'll go make that call to Maintenance."

He rolled the chair away from the desk and stood, easing out of the cramped space. She sucked in a breath at the solid, familiar feel of him as his chest and one of his thighs rubbed against her, slower than seemed necessary, on his way by. He smelled of man soap. Tangy. Delicious.

She could taste the memory of him on the tip of her tongue.

Once he was gone and had closed the office door behind him, her legs gave out. She dropped into the chair he'd vacated.

This Logan was so different from the man she'd met in Ottawa. He was more controlled and intense and less open. She couldn't decide if he was playing with her or not.

If he wanted to believe Olivia wasn't his, then she'd let him. But if he was interested in learning about her, he was going to have to ask. She wouldn't volunteer any information.

And if he was trying to pick up where they'd left off two years ago, he was wasting his time. She had no intentions of continuing that particular game. Not with Logan.

Not with Olivia now part of the stakes.

Chapter Six

Cass was right. A commissionaire on rounds would notice if anyone was in her office after hours. They simply might not think it was worth making note of, at least on paper.

After he called Maintenance, Logan went down to the security desk at the main entrance. The commissionaire on duty right now wouldn't have been working last night, but he should have a logbook containing the names of anyone entering the building after hours.

The commissionaire had his feet up on his desk and was reading a worn paperback. A lot of these guys were retired military or coast guard, sometimes from the reserves. They usually had a relaxed approach to their job and were reluctant to jump on every little thing that wasn't "by the book," but in Logan's experience, they noticed a lot. They simply picked their battles.

"Hey," Logan said.

"Hey, New Guy," the commissionaire replied. He swung

his feet to the worn tile floor, the regulation black boots landing with a solid *thud*. He set the open paperback face down on the desktop. "What can I do for you?"

Logan leaned on the counter above the desk. "Cass Stone's office was open this morning when she came in. She says it's the second time this week. It's most likely the cleaners, but I'm not sure who I report it to, you guys or Maintenance?"

"Both." The commissionaire reached for the logbook in front of him, shoved out of sight beneath the counter where Logan's elbows rested. "I'll check to see who's been working after hours, but it won't be much help. Her department's wide open to anyone inside the building."

The list of suspects now involved the entire company and not just the technical publications department. Worse, Logan discovered, the logbook didn't include anyone who'd stayed late to work extra hours, only those who came in after the main doors were locked for the night.

Cass claimed nothing had been taken. He'd seen no sign of unauthorized activity on her computer. This might have nothing to do with his investigation at all.

In the back of his head, a memory tweaked. When he'd first started working with CSIS, he'd read some of the old case files. One of the more experienced agents had drawn his attention to one case in particular. The individual charged had known from the start he'd get caught. He'd also been shrewd enough not to try and place the blame elsewhere. What he'd done instead was made every effort to pass his activities off as mischief, not outright theft, and he'd succeeded. A good lawyer had gotten him a dishonorable discharge instead of the jail time he'd deserved.

You want to make sure that little loophole is closed, the older agent had advised him. *Guys like this one are usually bitter about something. Maybe a promotion they didn't get. And they're smart. But bottom line? It's always about money. Anything else is an excuse.*

He went back upstairs to his own desk. He thought about the best way to get security cameras installed without anyone noticing and then had a better idea. An ordinary webcam from an office-supply store would work, too. If he angled the camera toward Cass's door, he should be able to get a clear image.

One of the writers came up to his desk with a sheath of papers in his hand. He tried to pass them to Logan. "I need you to send a fax for me."

Logan ignored the handful of papers. "Tell you what. I'll show you how to use the fax machine and you can send them yourself."

"You're the admin assistant," the writer said.

Logan tapped a notice labeled ATTENTION ALL STAFF taped to the wall above the fax machine. "I assume these step-by-step instructions aren't meant for Theresa. What would you do if you were working after hours and she wasn't here?"

"Never mind. I'll get Cass to do it for me." The writer snatched back the papers and stalked over to her door. He knocked once and opened it without waiting for any response.

Logan wondered how she'd handle this. She was supposed to be the department director. She wasn't going to get any respect by sending this fax, but she wouldn't earn any points by refusing. Talk about a rock and a hard place.

"Of course," he heard her say.

He had to admit, he was disappointed. Some sort of spanking might do her good. If he couldn't give her one, he'd been hoping this guy would at least raise her blood pressure.

Then she continued, "I have to finish these financial reports first. Can you come back in an hour? Oh. No, wait. I have a meeting with the other department heads in an hour. If you come back after lunch, I can fax them for you then."

The writer shifted from one foot to the other, his impatience obvious. "But these have to be in Ottawa right now. The captain is waiting for them."

"Sorry," she said, and Logan had to hand it to her, she sounded sincere. "But the VP of Finance is waiting for mine. You'd better see if Logan can help you out."

Well, well. He rubbed his chin. She'd managed that with more firmness and tact than he'd expected.

The writer returned to the reception desk and looked at him without saying anything.

"Put the documents facedown into the front paper feeder," Logan instructed him. "The one without any paper already in it. Punch in the fax number you want and hit the blue button to send."

The writer mumbled something under his breath that Logan chose to ignore, then once the fax was sent, grabbed his papers and stalked off toward his department.

A woman passed him in the hall, walking toward Logan with a wide smile on her face. She was short and blonde, slightly stocky, and maybe forty-five years old. She looked like a heavy smoker, or at least a former one.

"Hi," she said, giving him a slow, head-to-toe scan. "My name's Isabelle. I'm one of the writers. I need some things from the supply closet, but don't worry, I can get them myself."

"Nice try," he replied, grinning back. "But I fell for that one yesterday."

"It was worth a shot." Isabelle glanced over her shoulder to make sure the other writer was out of earshot. "Don't worry about Ivan. He's like that with everyone. He used to fly a Griffon."

Thanks to their personnel files, Logan already knew the backgrounds of everyone in the department. Griffon helicopters, underpowered for most military deployments, were generally considered a procurement mistake. That probably explained Ivan's need to assert his authority. With pilots, it was a bit like penis envy.

Isabelle Walsh, on the other hand, used to be a Sea King helicopter mechanic until she'd been sidelined by a bad back. Sea Kings were workhorses, with over fifty years in service and no equivalent replacement in sight. As a naval helicopter, the military loved them.

Both Ivan and Isabelle had good pensions that they were subsidizing with civilian work at Kramer Aerospace. Neither of them had anything in their backgrounds to trigger Logan's suspicions.

Isabelle leaned across the reception counter and waggled her eyebrows at him. "So. Handsome. What brings you to the company?"

"A temp agency and the right security clearances," he replied. He dug around in a drawer for the key to the supply closet. "What can I get for you?"

"Sticky notes and correction tape."

He opened the closet, found the yellow pads of paper

and the correction tape, and handed them to Isabelle. He was curious to find out what the staff really thought of Cass, and Isabelle was the perfect source of information—gossipy, entertaining, and no doubt a cougar.

He double-checked to make sure Cass's office door was still closed. "So what's Cass like as a boss? Anything I should know?"

"She's out of your league, Handsome. Don't get me wrong. She's nice enough, just too standoffish. And fancy," Isabelle added with a hint of disdain in her tone. "She has expensive tastes. But that's what really matters in this company. She's got the image Corporate wants to present, and she knows how to work it."

He didn't like hearing the expensive part. Professionally speaking—meaning his profession—it made him uneasy. "In what way is she expensive?"

Isabelle gave him a look that said he had to be either blind or stupid. "Her clothes. Her hair. She likes designer labels. Trendy salons." She leaned a little closer. "Rumor has it that someone in upper management's been…rewarding her."

He didn't like hearing that either. "Rewarding how?"

"It's not much of a secret that she got this promotion because one of the VPs knocked her up, and that Baxter Dempsey's the likeliest candidate. He certainly spends the most time with her. They do a lot of *lunches* together." Isabelle did that little "air quote" thing with her fingers. She gathered her office supplies. "Time to get back to work before my supervisor gets all tetchy. Talk to you later."

It seemed the bitterness angle wasn't going to be all that hard to investigate. So far he was two for two.

As he locked up the supply closet, he wondered why the office speculation about Cass bugged him so much. He knew who the father of her baby was. He also knew she wasn't sleeping with Dempsey. It was too obvious that Dempsey would like her to be for him to have scored.

But Logan couldn't say, with absolute certainty, whether or not she was the kind of woman to sleep her way to the top. Even though his gut told him no, he wasn't impartial.

When he thought of the way she'd behaved in Ottawa with the retired light colonel, the one who'd tried to ply her with alcohol, he couldn't see it. The Cass he'd watched that night had been eager to succeed, but also professional. She'd been excited about a work opportunity she'd been handed. She'd been very, very careful to keep her work separate from any celebrating she'd done, too. She hadn't wanted anyone to see her leaving the bar with the bartender.

Yet he'd been the one to call a halt to things in her kitchen last night.

And she'd kept Olivia a secret, not only from him, but everyone.

So, no. He couldn't safely say he knew anything about her, anymore. Or that he ever really had in the first place.

But he planned to find out.

...

Cass kicked the front door shut with the heel of her boot, thankful the long day was over. She tossed the keys of her newly repaired van into the dish on the sideboard next to the second story stairwell before wrestling Olivia's jacket off her wriggling, little body.

"No, no, no!" Olivia wailed at the top of her lungs, angry because she hadn't wanted to come inside so soon.

Cass was glad it was Friday. She and Olivia needed some serious mother-daughter time together. They'd be able to go to the park tomorrow after their errands.

"Come on, Livs," she coaxed. "We'll get into our jammies and listen to music while we eat dinner."

A short time later they were in the kitchen with the music on. Olivia was wearing a fuzzy pink onesie with bunny feet. Cass sported gray sweats and a pink tank under a white hoodie. She wore bunny slippers, too, because Olivia loved to poke at their eyes.

Cass was singing along to a children's *Razzmatazz* CD while she made dinner, making chicken noises for Olivia's entertainment, when someone knocked on the screen door.

She whirled, catching the ear of one floppy slipper on the leg of a chair. She fumbled with the chair to keep it from toppling over.

"Damn!" she swore under her breath.

"Damn!" Olivia echoed, but far louder and with more gusto.

Logan peered at them through the black screen mesh of the door.

"Raising a sailor, are we?" he asked, over the music.

Cass's heart hammered against her eardrums. The microwave timer dinged behind her.

"What are you doing here?" she asked.

"Collecting for the Red Cross." Cass stared at him. He held up a clipboard. "Seriously. I'm collecting for the Red Cross. Nan suckered me into it. Can I come in?"

She wanted to say no. She tugged at the hem of her white

hoodie, self-conscious and wishing she'd done something with her sloppy curls other than to scrape them up in a hair claw, but she'd been planning a girls' night in. No boys allowed.

Instead, she punched the off button on the CD player and unlatched the screen door.

He stepped into her kitchen, looking far better than he should in a chunky cream sweater and faded blue jeans. He held the clipboard in one hand and a receipt book in the other. He dropped them both onto the table, ignoring Cass completely as he brushed past her to crouch down on his heels in front of Olivia.

"I see your mother likes the color pink," he said to the toddler. "It doesn't go well at all with the language she's teaching you."

Olivia studied his face, her blue eyes wide, chubby cheeks quivering. For a second Cass thought—okay, a mean part of her hoped—she might burst into tears.

Instead, Olivia grabbed two fistfuls of his sweater and showed him her latest trick, which involved pulling herself to her feet while planting a slobbery kiss full on his lips. Then she stuck her tongue in his mouth.

Once he got over his surprise, he started to laugh. The look he shot Cass over Olivia's head was wicked and made her cheeks burn. Other places, too. "Wow. Your mother's been teaching you all kinds of useful things."

He lifted Olivia into his arms and stood up. Panic squeezed Cass's still-pounding heart. When they were together like that, with their faces side by side, they looked so much alike any idiot could see it.

Worse, there was something terribly sexy about a man

who held a baby as if he knew what he was doing.

Cass couldn't quite figure him out. Everything he did, he did well, and with confidence and self-assurance. Yet he had no ambition. He lived with his grandmother. And Cass still wouldn't mind if he…

So she guessed she couldn't figure herself out either.

She reached for her daughter, but Logan shifted away, blocking her with his shoulder so she couldn't take Olivia from him.

"You've had her all to yourself for a year and a half," he said. "It won't hurt you to share her with me for a few minutes. Besides, kids love me."

Even though Cass was starting to suspect that he never planned to broach the subject of Olivia head-on, there was an air of challenge to his light tone that she didn't dare poke.

She thought about the different ways she could play this situation. If he thought she was going to make some sort of confession—or worse, demands—that he didn't want to hear, then he could think again.

"What do you know about children?" she asked.

Olivia patted his face and he tickled her neck with his fingers in response, making her scrunch her chin and giggle. "I have two nephews, aged seven and eleven. I lived with them for a year after their dad died. I'm their favorite uncle." When he looked at Cass, his eyes were as unreadable as ever. "There's a lot about me you don't know. If you want to find out anything else, the information will cost you."

Those same nephews would be Olivia's cousins. A panicky sensation crawled up Cass's spine. Her life had been simpler before Logan showed up, ruining everything. She didn't want to know anything more about him.

"I already have all the information I need," she said. "You're a decent bartender and a good administrative assistant."

"Don't forget that I am *awesome* in bed."

He tugged at one of Olivia's dark curls as he spoke. She'd had enough of being held, however, and squirmed to get down, so he placed her on her bunny-clad feet, holding her under the arms of her fuzzy onesie until her legs steadied beneath her.

Cass sniffed. "You were okay. A little submissive, perhaps."

He froze for a fraction of a second. Then he straightened. A gleam entered his eyes as he looked straight into hers. A slow-burning, predatory smile tugged at the corners of his mouth and he took two steps toward her, shrinking the already small gap of space between them.

She took a half step back and bumped into the counter. And she remembered exactly, in vivid detail, why she'd been so attracted to him. He might not be bursting with ambition, but when it came to testosterone he'd been handed more than his share.

His breath brushed along her throat as he tipped his head closer. Pressing the palms of her hands against the cupboards behind her, bracing herself for his kiss, she shivered to the soles of her feet.

The kiss never came.

"As I recall," he said, his lips hovering scant inches from hers, "last time was lady's choice. If you'd like a do-over, pick your safe word."

She studied his chin. No way was she backing down first. "Safe words are for sissies."

He traced the tip of his finger down the side of her cheek and along the line of her neck, and she lost the ability to swallow.

"Maybe so," he said. "But unlike some people, I'm not into inflicting permanent emotional scars."

For some ridiculous reason, that made her insides smile. He remembered what she'd said to him the night they met, when she'd joked about celebrating her release from prison.

She felt a tug on one of her bunny slippers and looked down. Olivia sat on the floor at her feet, picking at one of the bunny's plastic beaded eyes, humming what sounded like a laundry-detergent commercial.

When she glanced up, Cass caught an odd expression, almost of pain, crossing Logan's face. Just as quickly, it was gone.

So was any desire Cass had to smile. That comment about emotional scarring he'd made didn't seem quite so funny to her when she put it in a different context.

He was interested in Olivia. She'd bet her new minivan on it. But for whatever reason, he wasn't planning to acknowledge she was his daughter.

He put some space back between them. Cass groped for the microwave on the counter behind her. She needed to think, and she couldn't do that with him in her kitchen.

"If you don't mind," she said, "I was about to give Olivia her dinner. Can I write you a check?"

He looked puzzled for a split second until his gaze landed on the clipboard and receipt book he'd dropped in the middle of her kitchen table. His face cleared. Then he smiled again, crease lines embracing his mouth, and she decided she'd read too much into his wordplay. For the life of her, she couldn't figure him out. It was driving her crazy.

"Of course you can write a check," he said. "But go ahead and feed Olivia first. I'll make myself a cup of tea while I wait. And now it's my turn to ask you a question." Her confusion must have shown on her face. "I told you if you wanted to find out anything more from me, the information would cost you. You asked if you can write me a check. The answer's yes."

"You can't be serious," she said.

He'd already picked up her electric kettle from its place by the ceramic stove and was filling it at the sink. Water gushed from the brushed stainless-steel faucet. He nudged the faucet off and plugged in the kettle. "Oh, I'm very serious. Don't tell me you're chicken."

"No," she replied, triumphant. "There. I've answered a question. That makes us even." And she'd know better than to ask any more.

He'd helped her put away dishes after her impromptu birthday gathering, so he knew where she kept her cups and the tea. He reached into one of the cupboards. The china teacup he selected looked delicate in his long fingers as he held it, his movements arrested. His voice went soft. "We are so far from even, you can't begin to imagine. And that wasn't a question, Miss Mary. I said 'don't tell me,' not 'spill your guts.' I want to know about your family. Do you have any, other than Olivia?"

The question threw her. By the way he was acting she'd thought he would ask something about Olivia.

She wanted to shock him. To shake all that confidence. Because she'd never had a grandmother's sofa to crash on. There'd been no safety net for her.

She lifted Olivia into her high chair and fastened her in, then picked her words carefully, not wanting to sound pitiful or bitter, because she wasn't. Her father couldn't help what he was. She didn't want him in Olivia's life, anyway. Her mother and sisters were a different matter, but any estrangement was their choice, not hers. If they ever developed some backbone and changed their minds, she'd welcome them.

She got Olivia's dinner from the microwave and sat in a chair beside her, dipping a silicone-tipped spoon into the soft green mush in the bowl.

"I have parents and three sisters, but we haven't spoken in years," she said to him. "My father told me I was too wild, and to be honest, I can't say he was wrong. I was smart and pretty independent as a teenager, and thought I knew everything, but I never put too much thought into consequences. He said I was a bad influence on my younger sisters and ordered me to stay away from them all. So really, as far as family, Olivia's it."

The kettle started to sing. He didn't seem to notice. Cass couldn't read him, and that both fascinated and frustrated her. She knew exactly why she'd gone after him in that hotel bar, and it wasn't because of his looks. She'd sensed a challenge and hadn't been able to resist. It seemed she still couldn't. Her palms were sweating.

Definitely no thought put into consequences.

"How old were you when he turned you out?" he asked.

"I'd just turned eighteen. Although I'd run away for five months when I was fifteen, so it was anticlimactic. I hadn't planned to go back then, but Social Services had other ideas." She tried to keep things light, even though her lips felt funny and stiff when she spoke. She didn't talk much about her family. "That was another question, so now it's my turn to ask you one."

The singing switched to a high-pitched, insistent whistle, then the kettle shut itself off. Olivia opened her mouth wide, grabbing for the spoon in Cass's hand.

He ignored the comment about it being her turn to ask a question. Instead, he searched for the tea and a little ceramic pot that was hidden in a corner. His fingers closed around the white handle.

"I'm sorry," he finally said, speaking to the teapot because he had his back to her. "I didn't realize."

Cass wondered why it was, considering she and Logan had done some pretty intimate things together, that conversation between them always turned out so awkward. Then again, she'd intentionally set out to make things that way.

She should never have played along with his stupid Q & A game, and saw little point in encouraging him further.

She was done playing games. Her wild days were over. She wasn't wasting her time trying to figure him out. As soon as the regular executive assistant returned from her emergency Logan would be gone and most likely for good. In the meantime, she didn't want him thinking he could come over here any time and see Olivia, even though Olivia was too young to become attached to him.

Because Cass had a feeling she wasn't.

Chapter Seven

Cass came with baggage.

As Logan poured hot water over the tea bag in the pot, he wondered why that surprised him so much. And why it made him feel like such a jerk for tormenting her with a silly game.

If not for his sister, and the brother-in-law who deserved justice from the government he'd served, he knew he'd walk away from his assignment this minute. He and Cass needed to work some things out, most especially with regard to Olivia.

Because no way was he walking away from that. His daughter was beautiful. She was wonderful. She was covered in mashed peas, and what looked like either ground chicken or pork, and he'd never seen anything more adorable in his life.

Cass in those bunny slippers, with those long, bouncy curls flopping into her gorgeous hazel eyes, came a close second. She had a tiny blob of food crusted on the left sleeve of her white hoodie. He found that particularly fascinating because it was so out of character with the appearance-conscious woman he'd studied all day.

He blinked rapidly a few times, carefully keeping his back turned to her, and worked on pouring the stupid tea that he wasn't sure he could swallow without choking.

He wanted to be a part of his daughter's life so bad he was willing to say the hell with his work. Let someone else find whoever was selling the secrets. But if he walked away now, and another CSIS agent tried to move into that publications department, it wouldn't be long before the guilty party got skittish.

Olivia had a father. She didn't know him yet, but someday she would. His nephews, on the other hand, would never get their father back. Logan owed it to other kids to see that their dads came home.

Cass's cellphone rang.

He abandoned the tea, practically snatching the bowl and spoon from her hands, then nudged her out of the way with his hip so he could take over feeding Olivia.

She gave in and answered the phone, but kept her eyes on him as if ready to interfere at the first sign of incompetence on his part.

He scooped a bit of the magic meat mixture off Olivia's plump bottom lip with the side of the spoon, then flashed her a thumbs-up sign before popping the spoon into Olivia's puckered-up mouth.

He was having fun, watching her roll her food around on her tongue before squirting it out the corners of her lips, until he caught Cass's side of the phone conversation.

She was agreeing to go out this Saturday night with the brother of some friend named Patricia.

Hot, searing pain lanced his chest.

He popped the last sloppy spoonful of dinner into Olivia's mouth and wiped her face with the cleanest spot he could find on her bib. He inspected her for damage. No food on the cute little pink onesie. She was good to go. He unstrapped her and lifted her from the high chair, holding her for a moment until the ache in his chest subsided enough for him to breathe without passing out.

He wasn't jealous over the thought of Cass and another man, but he hated the possibility of Olivia calling someone else daddy.

Cass was still watching him as she hit the off button on her phone with her thumb.

"I'll write that check now," she said.

She scrabbled around in a kitchen drawer for a pen and her checkbook. Then she bent over the table and wrote out the donation.

He enjoyed the view as the band of those thin, hip-hugging gray sweatpants parted ways with the hem of her hoodie, exposing cream-colored flesh and two strips of white lace, one horizontal, the other vertical. His eyes tracked the path of that vertical line. The last thong he'd seen her wear had been fire-engine red.

If anything, he thought he liked those bunny slippers the best. He changed his mind. Yes, he was jealous over the thought of Cass and another man.

Top that with her being his boss, and him investigating her company, and this entire situation had *clusterfuck* written all over it.

He had to back off.

"Need a babysitter tomorrow night?" he heard himself say.

She tugged the bottom of her hoodie back into place. A thick, corkscrew curl sprang free, draping over her eye to tickle the tip of her nose. She tucked it behind her ear. "I don't think that's such a good idea."

"We've established how good I am with children."

"It doesn't matter how good you are at feeding her dinner. I can't leave my young daughter alone with a strange man."

She hadn't said that to be cruel, and it was a valid concern, but having her think for a second that he might somehow harm Olivia cut deep. The more reluctant she proved to be, the harder he had to push. It was like she'd waved a red flag.

"Nan would love to help out with Olivia. She's not a stranger." His grandmother was too old to be left alone with a toddler, but between the two of them, they'd manage fine.

Cass frowned. She folded her arms across her chest and met his gaze with her best *I'm the boss* stare. "Why would you want to babysit a little girl you don't even know?"

She was putting it out there. Sounding him out to see how he'd react. If he was ready to step up. Man up. His palms went damp.

Because she's mine and I love her already, he wished he could say.

But he loved his nephews, too. And he wanted to look himself in the mirror each morning and know he'd done the right thing.

Olivia nestled her diaper-clad bottom into the crook of his elbow. She dropped her head to his shoulder and stuck her thumb in her mouth. The fluff of her soft, baby curls brushed the underside of his jaw. She smelled like baby powder, apple juice, and mashed peas. He tried to block out all the wonderful, but it was hard.

"Kids are great when they're somebody else's problem," he said with a careless shrug. "They're cute and fun to play with, and best of all, you can hand them back when they need braces."

His throat ached from forcing those words out of his mouth, and the look of disappointment on Cass's face flung them back to grind into his skin like bits of crushed glass. She was going to say no, and he couldn't say that he blamed her.

"Who do you usually get to babysit?" he pressed. "What if she isn't available on such short notice?"

Cass hesitated. "She's available. She has a little boy not much older than Olivia. They go to daycare together."

"This is the same friend who's fixing you up with her brother, isn't it?" he guessed.

She dropped her hands to her hips, her eyes turning to bone-chilling ice. A lesser man would have been frozen to death on the spot.

He held up one palm in a warding-off motion. "I'm not interfering. All I'm trying to point out is that it might prove awkward for you. What if the date goes south and she asks for details? What if the brother turns out to be a real loser?"

Her eyes narrowed and her lips thinned. "You mean like a former bartender turned admin assistant who lives with his grandmother?"

He might deserve that, but it was still a low blow.

He shrugged. "It's not like you picked this guy up in a

bar. It'll be a lot harder to pretend you never slept with him if you're friends with his sister."

She slapped the check into his free hand as if she wished it were his face and reached for Olivia. "Give me my daughter."

He did, but not willingly.

Olivia didn't want to go either. She had one tiny fist curled into the sleeve of his sweater, and Cass had to pry her fingers loose.

Logan stood there in Cass's kitchen, empty-handed and desperate, and stared at his beautiful, sleepy-eyed daughter and her equally beautiful, really pissed off, mother. And he wanted them both so bad that his gut ached.

He crammed the check into the pocket of his jeans.

"Please, Cass," he said, begging now and not the least bit ashamed of it. "Let me look after her for you."

Conflict played out on her face. She was going to say no. He could feel it, and braced himself for rejection even as his mind began spinning, searching for a good argument that might somehow sway her.

"Okay," she said. "But just this once."

• • •

Saturday morning arrived, warm, fresh, and clear.

Cass crammed the diaper bag into the rear of the minivan, next to the stroller. Olivia waited patiently in her car seat, playing with the toes of her sneakers.

Cass knew she shouldn't have agreed to let Logan babysit tonight but she'd seen the desperate longing on his face that, for whatever reason, he refused to admit. She'd said yes because she'd never once seen that look on her own father's face. Logan might lack ambition, and it was obvious to her that he didn't want any responsibility for Olivia, but he wasn't heartless, or cold and judgmental.

She didn't want to be that way either. When Olivia asked about her father, as she inevitably would, Cass would like to be able to say in all honesty that she'd never tried to keep them apart.

It was the shock of discovering that Olivia had cousins and a great aunt, and how many more relatives so far uncounted, however, that had really decided things for Cass in the end. Her family hadn't wanted Olivia.

Maybe someday, after Logan made up his own mind about her, his family would. It was his call to make.

Mrs. Sheridan, her empty grocery bags hooked over one arm, pushed through the hole in the hedge, right on time. Behind her came Logan, looking tall, dark, and handsome.

"Ethel can't make it this morning," his grandmother announced. "That leaves room for Logan. He wanted to come. I hope you don't mind," she added.

Cass could hardly say that she did.

"You like grocery shopping?" she asked him.

He jiggled his fingers at Olivia through the van's open side door, and was rewarded with a happy, baby-toothed grin. "I had nothing better to do."

"Your grandmother has storm windows that need to be removed. And her garage needs to be cleaned out. She's been talking about them for weeks." Cass took a wicked pleasure in pointing the chores out. Let him earn his room and board.

Mrs. Sheridan answered for him, hands fluttering in the

air like a nervous little bird's wings. "Logan's too busy for that," she rushed to assure her. "I'd rather enjoy his visit. I don't see as much of him as I'd like anymore."

He didn't have the decency to be embarrassed about freeloading. The message Cass got instead was one of self-satisfaction. He was used to getting whatever he wanted. Since she had a history of giving in to him, too, she could hardly criticize his grandmother for spoiling him. The man was a manipulator.

But a harmless one. And he could be charming.

He knocked a clump of dirt he'd picked up from the hedge off his running shoe before helping his grandmother into the front passenger seat of the van. Cass half thought he might try to take the driver's seat for himself, but instead, he climbed into the back so he could sit beside Olivia. He slid over close enough to sling an arm along the seat behind her, and she chattered to him as she showed off her sippy cup.

Cass's heart thumped triple time. She wondered if his grandmother would notice the resemblance between them. All Mrs. Sheridan had to do was turn her head and look.

"What are we waiting for?" he asked, glancing over his shoulder and meeting Cass's eyes as she stood at the back of the van.

She heard the unspoken *Miss Mary* tagged on at the end, and caught the challenge in his eyes. He knew what she was thinking and what she was afraid of, and he planned to use it against her.

She slammed the hatch door. She didn't know why, or what he hoped to gain, but whatever he was up to, she couldn't let this challenge go unanswered.

The first stop was the nursing home so Mrs. Sheridan

could visit her friend, Mrs. Calaveccio, the woman Cass had bought her house from. Mrs. Calaveccio didn't know Cass—most days, she couldn't remember Mrs. Sheridan—so Cass never went in. She always drove up to the main door, let any passengers out, and then took Olivia to the park for an hour.

He helped his grandmother out of the van. When he went to follow her inside, she stopped him with a pat on his arm.

"Thank you for the thought, but I'm fine on my own. Why don't you go to the park with Cass and Olivia?" she said.

Cass eavesdropped without shame.

"I haven't seen Mrs. Calaveccio in years," he replied.

"Mabel wouldn't want you to see her the way she is now," Mrs. Sheridan said gently. "Keep your memories. Go have fun with the girls."

He stood as if undecided about what he should do until his grandmother made a shooing motion with her hands. He watched her as she walked through the twin sliding glass doors, straight-backed and dignified, in no need of assistance. When he got back in the van, he climbed into the front beside Cass.

To Cass, he seemed shaken. He didn't say anything so neither did she, but as she drove away from the nursing home, her heart melted.

The park where she took Olivia on Saturdays was a few short blocks over. She found a spot for the van on the street with no trouble.

"Can you get the stroller?" she asked him as she unbuckled Olivia from her seat.

"Let's leave the stroller behind." He rolled his shoulders

as if his muscles were stiff. "I'll carry her when she gets tired."

Cass didn't argue. Instead, she admired his patience as he held Olivia's hand and let the toddler wobble on her own through the wrought iron gates. She hadn't planned to allow this level of interaction. Olivia would be in bed by the time he came over to sit with her this evening. But the two of them looked so cute together she couldn't resist watching without interfering.

Logan looked back, seeing that she'd lagged a little behind. His eyes were brilliant blue sparks of light in the bright morning sun. They held the same glint of humor and warmth that had made her notice him when they first met, and she fell a little harder.

"Race you to the duck pond, Miss Mary," he said.

She should tell him to stop calling her that, but he was after a reaction and she wouldn't give him one.

She held up the diaper bag. "If you win, it'll be a hollow victory. I have the bird seed."

The light danced in his eyes, his lips twitching with open good humor. "We can't have that."

He reached for her with his free hand, taking her fingers in his. The world disappeared, leaving nothing but the heat of the sun and the touch of his skin on hers. This was inappropriate for so many reasons, and wrong for so many more. She had too much to lose by letting him close. And yet she couldn't make herself step away.

Hand in hand, they walked the path through the park toward the duck pond. Every few feet Olivia discovered wonderful new things at her eye level, and Logan would stop to examine them with her—a flower, a bug, a pretty-colored rock. Cass wondered why she'd never thought to let

Olivia walk on her own before, but knew it was because she didn't have his level of patience. Until Olivia was born she'd had none to speak of at all. Cass was Type A, no question about it.

While Logan…

He was Type B, through and through.

• • •

Logan couldn't decide which one of them to watch as they fed bird seed to the ducks—his daughter or Cass. Both stole his breath—Cass because she was so smart and beautiful, and Olivia, well. She was plain wonderful. So he compromised and watched them both.

His attraction to Cass hadn't changed, and he was confident she felt the same way, but he was impatient for her to get to know him for who he really was. Despite her apparent contempt for low-income earners, he was no different as a bartender or an admin assistant than he was as a CSIS agent.

And he planned to be the best father ever.

Whenever the ducks became too aggressive, Logan swooped Olivia off her feet and out of the way, swinging her high in the air. She squealed with laughter, unafraid. She'd inherited her mom's fearlessness and sense of adventure.

She'd be a teenager someday. Then, their hands would be full. That thought made him feel old, which in turn, reminded him of how much his grandmother had aged. She should have more family close by. It was great to have friends who cared the way Mrs. Calaveccio's did, but none of them were getting any younger. They couldn't look after each other forever.

"What's wrong?" Cass asked, and he lost his train of thought when he realized that she'd been studying him as closely as he'd been watching her, only with a bit more discreetness.

"Not a thing." He helped Olivia toss the last handful of feed, cupping her tiny fist in his hand and giving her extra thrust. "Just imagining the fireworks when she turns sixteen."

Cass picked up the diaper bag, which she'd dropped on the mulchy, pine-needle-carpeted ground, and slung it over her shoulder. She dusted the residue from the bird seed sticking to her palms onto the thighs of her jeans. "You think I can't handle a teenage girl?"

He held up his hands in surrender. "I never said that."

"That's okay," Cass said. "I'm dreading it, too. She's already a handful when she makes up her mind about something."

He looked at Olivia, who was happily poking her fingers in the dirt and singing something unidentifiable to herself. He'd seen her in action before, the first time he'd met her in front of Cass's house, so he wasn't surprised. Besides, she was creeping up on the terrible twos.

"It's got to be something you're doing wrong," he said. "She seems pretty easygoing to me."

"You think?" Cass's eyebrows lifted. "Hold onto that image for two more seconds." She made a show of checking her watch. "Come on Livs, it's time to go."

Olivia plopped her diapered bottom onto the ground and started to cry.

He shook his head. "I'm appalled. What did you expect? You didn't finesse it. Where are your leadership skills? You have to frame what you want her to do in a more positive way. Let her play a part in the decision."

He crouched down beside Olivia. She was now wailing in earnest, and he let her work out her tantrum for a minute or so. Then he said, "Olivia, honey, would you like to come with me to see more birds by the gate?"

"Those are pigeons," Cass said, with that same inflection she used whenever she mentioned his job.

The one that annoyed him.

"To you, they're nothing special. To her, a bird is a bird."

As if to prove it, Olivia stopped crying.

"Okay," Cass said. "But you also have to get her into the car seat." She held up one finger to keep him from interrupting. "And you have to do it without any screaming."

This was like taking candy from a baby. He wasn't his nephews' favorite uncle for nothing. "That sounds like a challenge. If I can do it, what's my reward?"

She got a cautious look in her eyes. Then her daredevil streak intervened. "What do you want?"

"I want to know why you chose engineering."

He watched her examine his request, turning it over in her head as if trying to find some dark, hidden agenda. Miss Mary wasn't the trusting sort.

He wasn't worried. He really was curious about her, but knew better than to chase too much information too soon.

"You're on," she said.

Olivia had lost interest in walking by now, so he carried her back to the gate. When they got to it, he didn't stop. He didn't even slow down.

"See the birds, Olivia?" he asked her as they walked past six or seven pigeons strutting around on the sidewalk outside the gate.

She watched them from over his shoulder while Cass unlocked the van. Once it was open, he jiggled Olivia, bouncing her on his arm to regain her attention. "Where's your sippy cup?"

Olivia looked around, saw it was in her seat, and reached for it. A minute later, he had her fastened in.

When he straightened, triumphant, Cass had her hands on her hips.

"This is why I don't gamble," she said, but he could tell he'd impressed her. "I chose engineering because I like math, and I like figuring out how to make things work. Plus, my university advisor told me an engineering degree was a fast track to management for women in business."

She continued to surprise him. On the one hand, she set goals and planned for her future. On the other, she didn't let opportunities for fun pass her by.

Logan had liked her already. More and more, he admired her.

So, while he was thrilled he'd be getting to spend the whole evening with Olivia, he was growing less excited about that blind date all the time.

Something of what he was feeling must have shown on his face as he took the passenger seat.

"What's wrong?" Cass asked, pausing in the act of latching her seat belt.

Everything he could think of. He said the first thing that popped into his head. "I failed high school physics."

Her eyes sparkled, showing off the humor he'd loved so much about her.

"Don't worry, you're too pretty to need it," she said, and

he laughed.

In the backseat, Olivia made a coughing noise, as if she were choking. Both Cass and Logan turned around at the same time. Their shoulders brushed, bringing their faces closer together.

The coughing stopped. A trickle of juice dripped off Olivia's puckered lower lip. Cass settled back, about to take her seat again, when acting on impulse, he reached up and wrapped a handful of her curls around his fingers. He tugged her toward him, sliding his free hand around her waist. She rested one palm on his shoulder as if to steady herself.

Or perhaps, to push him away.

If so she'd had second thoughts, because when he kissed her, she didn't resist. His fingers tightened in her hair. Desire exploded through his chest, setting off fireworks that by rights should have toppled the van. This was the side of her he remembered so well, the one full of passion and life, and willing to seize opportunity with both hands.

He kept the kiss brief, over almost before it began, so as not to give the more practical, suspicious side of her too much time to analyze his motives. The street was quiet, but they were in a public place, in front of a popular city park. He didn't want to embarrass her, or to push her too hard too soon. In Ottawa, there had been very little at stake for either one of them, really.

Now they both stood to lose things they valued.

She tidied her hair with one hand, looking flustered and cautious, and perhaps a little guilty. Inside, he smiled. He couldn't help but be pleased that he made her forget who was boss.

Let her take that on her date.

"Thank you, Miss Mary," he said.

Her eyes widened, then narrowed. "For what?"

"For being so kind to my grandmother and her friends."

He thought he caught disappointment in her eyes before she looked away, but that might be wishful thinking on his part. She reached for the key in the ignition and started the engine.

"They're kind to me, too," she said, and pulled the van away from the curb.

Chapter Eight

Spending the morning with Olivia and Logan made Cass's date preparations feel weird, like she was cheating on them, which was foolish.

She stood in front of her bedroom mirror, smoothing the fire-engine-red dress over her hips, and decided she'd pass inspection for an evening of drinks at the Fireside Lounge. The night outside was dry and mild so she'd opted to wear sleeveless, despite the stiff wind rattling the twin, single-pane windows.

She'd left her hair loose because she rarely got to wear it that way anymore, and it fell around her bare shoulders in shining, brushed-gold ringlets. She stretched one curl out, a nervous habit she had, and noticed with a start that the lock of hair reached well past her elbow.

Between work and a baby, she couldn't remember the last time she'd had a decent cut. Yet she could say, right to the hour and the day, the last time she'd been in bed with a man.

And to the exact second, the last time she'd been kissed. She made a face at herself in the mirror as she let the curl spring back into place.

The master bedroom, while shabby, and last on her long list of repairs, ran the full width of the front of the house. Streetlights streamed through the tall, narrow windows, splashing warmth across the wide-planked, bare pine floor. She'd sprung for a king-size bed when she'd moved in, more because it suited the dimensions of the room than out of any plans for double occupancy. When she'd bought the house, she'd had thoughts for no one but Olivia.

She opened the closet door and looked at the six shelves of shoes it contained. She hoped Patricia's brother was tall because low heels would ruin the flared line of her skirt. Not to mention her favorite black, three-inch peep toes hadn't seen the inside of a restaurant in months.

A motorcycle purred on the street outside. She could hear it gearing down as it took the corner. It slowed in front of her house. She looked out a window, lifting a sheer curtain panel with a finger, and watched as it pulled into Mrs. Sheridan's driveway next door.

Logan dismounted, swinging his knee over the low seat as he unfastened his helmet. He wore a dark brown leather jacket and faded jeans, and he spiked a hand through his hair in an effort to tidy it. He glanced up, the motion arrested as his gaze zeroed in on where she was watching him, and she let the panel drop. She backed hastily away from the window.

Logan was funny and smart, and good with Olivia.

He was good with Cass, too. She wished she were staying in, not going out, and it didn't help that she knew what she was missing. If she could turn the clock back two years, she'd still take that one night with him. In a heartbeat. She'd use the same sketchy condoms, too, because she didn't regret Olivia either.

It was because of Olivia, however, that tonight she'd chosen to listen to her practical side that told her to give Patricia's brother a chance.

But he had a tough act to follow.

She snagged her shoes, her clutch, and her jacket, and dashed down the stairs.

Logan stood at the kitchen door with his helmet tucked under one arm like a football.

Cass held her finger to her lips as she opened the door for him. "Olivia's already asleep."

Disappointment flashed across his face, disappearing with lightning speed, but she was learning what signs to read.

"I'll watch television," he said.

She bit her lip as she stepped aside to let him in. "The television is in my bedroom."

He set the helmet on the floor beside the door and slung his jacket over the back of one chair. He tilted his head sideways to look at her, one eyebrow raised. "I'm not going to ask why. I'm going to make assumptions."

She wanted to laugh, but she didn't want to encourage him. The thought of him in her bedroom was already too much.

"You could read a book instead," she suggested.

"Yeah? Whatcha got, Miss Mary? Because I have this sneaking suspicion your reading taste these days runs toward studying things like *key performance indicators*. And not for the fun performances."

Cass made a show of checking her watch rather than matching wits with some smartass rejoinder. With a start, she realized she was going to be late if she didn't hurry. "I've got to go."

"Your friend's brother isn't picking you up?" he asked.

She slipped her shoes on her feet. "I'd rather meet on neutral territory. I don't invite strange men to my house."

She waited for him to say it. *Just to your hotel room.*

But he didn't. He simply smiled at her with a soft, gentle expression in his eyes that warmed her all over, and then he took her jacket from her and held it so she could slide her arms into the sleeves. His knuckles brushed against her bare shoulders, trailing prickles of heat in their wake. "You look really beautiful, Cass."

His breath tracked the length of her neck like a lingering kiss. For a second, lost in the thrill of his touch, Cass couldn't move.

Tough act, indeed.

"Thank you," she finally managed to say. "If you need anything, my cell number is on the fridge. Olivia can have a drink of water if she wakes up, and a few crackers from the cupboard above the stove, but she usually sleeps through the night."

Cass fled, her feet tapping down the front steps to the pounding beat of her heart.

As she drove downtown, then searched for a parking spot that wasn't too far from the restaurant for her to walk in her heels, she tried to think. Her heart tugged her toward Logan. Her head said she was stupid. Both agreed that this date had been a mistake.

She wasn't ready.

She parked half a block from the restaurant. By the time she walked inside, she was fifteen minutes late.

She gave her name to a waitress, who led her to an easy chair by the fire in the lounge. A tall man with blond hair, and wearing an impeccable gray suit, stood up at her approach. This had to be Patricia's brother, David, the surgeon. They shared similar features.

He had tall and good-looking working in his favor. Success, it seemed, too.

She took the firm hand he offered. "I'm so sorry I'm late. I had babysitter trouble."

"No problem at all. I completely understand." David smiled, showing teeth that had to be orthodontist corrected. They were perfect. "Tricia said you have a little girl."

At least that subject was out of the way.

David turned out to be easy company. He was well-educated, well-traveled, and well-read. He asked polite questions about her career. He steered clear of anything too personal.

After the first half hour, Cass found him boring. He told her several times how pretty she looked, then scanned the room as if seeking someone he knew. It took her a while to realize he liked to be seen.

She wasn't certain she liked that in a date. When Logan looked at her, she felt as if she had his full attention. She didn't get the same sense from David.

If he'd been tending bar at the hotel in Ottawa, her key card would have stayed in her pocket.

"Tell me about your daughter," David said. He took a sip of his martini, eyeing her over the rim of his glass. "Is her father still in the picture?"

She'd thought long and hard about how she'd handle this question after she'd decided to start dating again. She didn't plan to give all the details, certainly not on a first date—maybe never—but she didn't intend to lie about it either.

"There isn't a father. Olivia and I are alone."

"We all make mistakes," David said.

For some inexplicable reason that casual response, even though she'd heard no judgment in it, irritated the hell out of her. Olivia was the best thing to ever happen to her. And Logan wasn't a bad person. At least he was genuine. To have them both classified as mistakes made her burn with an indignation she hadn't felt since she'd gotten the note from her father telling her to keep her bastard to herself.

David, as nice as he seemed, wasn't coming across as the kind of man who'd ever understand her need to assert her independence from a dominating father when she was younger. Not the way Logan had. She might have been wild, and she still enjoyed taking risks—although these days, they took place in the boardroom—but she'd never done anything she'd truly regretted.

She didn't plan to start now. For her, the evening was over.

She was driving, so she ordered a coffee instead of a second drink.

As soon as she thought it polite, she looked at her watch. "I told the babysitter I'd be home by eleven."

David made a small sound of disappointment, then rose when she did. He thanked her for a lovely evening. He suggested they try it again sometime, and kissed her goodbye on the cheek when she refused his offer to walk her to her car.

Cass, once she was out on the street, breathed a sigh of relief. She could tell Patricia what a nice man her brother was. David could tell his sister anything he liked. They'd both be off the hook.

But she could hardly go home before midnight. That would be the same as admitting to Logan that her date had gone south, as he'd predicted. Besides, he was partly to blame for its failure.

Cass went for a long drive along the coastline outside of Cornwall instead.

Shortly after midnight, she let herself into the house. The downstairs was so dark and silent, for a second, she panicked. What if something had happened to Olivia?

From there, her mother imagination went wild. What if they were both gone? What if this had all been a trick on Logan's part so he could gain her trust and steal Olivia away from her?

She took off her shoes and tiptoed quietly up the stairs, guided by the faint light above the stove in the kitchen that seeped through the open doorway and into the front entry.

Olivia's crib was empty.

Cass's panic spread from her chest to her limbs, turning her whole body into a numb, shivering and shaking mess. Then she heard a slight mumble of noise from her bedroom and realized the television was on.

She went to the open door. The fifty-five inch HD Smart television she should have known no man could resist cast a white, flickering glow across the foot of the king-size bed. Logan lay on top of the bright, quilted spread, his head propped against the pillows, his long legs stretched out and crossed at the ankles. He had the remote in one hand. Olivia sprawled across his chest, her thumb in her mouth, covered by the baby blanket from her crib. They were both sound asleep.

Tears filled Cass's eyes, both of relief and something less easily defined. They looked too adorable for words, and she couldn't bring herself to disturb them.

She leaned against the doorjamb and watched them sleep. When her feet finally grew cold from standing too long on the creaky plank flooring, she pattered downstairs, stripped off her pantyhose, and drifted off to sleep under the throw on the sofa in the front room.

...

A tiny finger poked at Logan's nose.

He peeled one eye open. Sunshine poured through the tall windows of a vaguely familiar, utterly feminine, if somewhat rundown, room. The television was on, its volume muted. Olivia bounced on the bed beside him, pink-cheeked and mussy-haired, a wide, baby-toothed grin on her face.

He fell more in love with his daughter. Someone certainly woke up in a good mood in the morning.

Morning.

He shot straight up in bed. What the hell had happened to Cass?

His thoughts went two places at once. Either the date had turned out to be a crazed serial killer, or she'd spent the night with him. He scooped Olivia into his arms and swung his feet to the floor, intending to run downstairs to get her cell number off the fridge door, when he heard what sounded like a pan clatter in the kitchen.

His worry subsided. The date hadn't been a serial killer, or if so, at least he hadn't murdered Cass. That left his second primary fear. Where had she spent the night?

He held Olivia tighter. It was none of his business. But it sure as hell was his daughter's.

Cass looked up from the stove when he stalked into the kitchen with Olivia in his arms. She'd already dropped two slices of French toast onto a hot griddle. The smile on her face faded when she took note of the expression on his.

"Where have you been?" he asked.

She wore the same dress she'd had on last night. And she looked every bit as beautiful as she had when she'd walked out the door, except she'd lost the shoes and nylons. The sight of those mile-long bare legs drove him nuts.

She knew it, too.

Her smile returned, brighter this time, and mixed with a touch of pure evil. "Best first date ever. We robbed a bank at gunpoint. After that, we checked into the Westin Hotel and played sex games all night. I was an illegal French maid. He was an immigration officer. Good call on not getting his sister to babysit, by the way. That would totally have been an awkward night to explain."

Olivia got her morning cheerfulness from her mother. He didn't try to analyze the monumental sense of relief that he felt, he simply rolled with it.

"Nice try," he said. "No banks were open last night. And I don't believe for a second you'd ever play a French maid. You came home early, found Olivia and me asleep in your bed, and crashed on the sofa."

"It wasn't all that early." She hooked her curls behind one ear and flipped the bread on the griddle. "Do you like your French toast with powdered sugar or maple syrup?"

He was getting breakfast. Now he knew for certain nothing more than conversation had happened last night. She wouldn't want to sit across the table from him if she'd slept with another man. Cass could never be that cold.

That was what his gut told him, at any rate.

"Syrup," he said.

She gave Olivia a plastic bowl filled with dry Cheerios and a sippy cup of apple juice. Olivia played with a sliced-up banana in her highchair while they ate breakfast. When they were finished, he helped wash the dishes.

Cass put the last clean plate in the cupboard.

"I need to get showered and dress Olivia," she said. "She could use a fresh diaper."

Logan liked to think he could take a hint. He'd asked to babysit for one evening, not move in. She'd already fed him breakfast, which was way more than he'd expected.

"I don't suppose you could give me a ride to work tomorrow?" he asked. "The bike's making a funny noise, and I don't want to borrow Nan's car more than I have to. No need to rack up the mileage and depreciate its value."

She got an odd look on her face that told him, for a tiny window of time, she'd forgotten she was, for all intents and purposes, his boss.

"What kind of noise is the bike making?"

And he'd forgotten she was an engineer. He scrambled for an ominous noise she'd believe. "It sounds like a rattling chain in the gearbox."

"Of course I can give you a lift." She paused as if she had something more she wanted to say, thought better, then decided to go for it. "Thank you for babysitting. But it might be best if we don't make a habit of this. You work in my office. You aren't my personal assistant and private nanny."

Stiff fingers pinched his heart. He read that to mean, *Don't think you have free access to Olivia and me any time you feel like it.*

He'd done a lot of thinking while he'd watched television with Olivia last night. First, he'd had to get past the last bits of angry frustration that he'd missed his daughter's first words, her first tooth, her first steps. Then he'd tried to see things from Cass's perspective.

She had her life right where she believed she wanted it, and he was the weak rung on her corporate ladder. He was an embarrassment to her. He'd already known that. But more than that, she was afraid he'd hurt Olivia because her own father had sucked. He'd seen how she looked when she spoke about being kicked out of his house. She'd worked hard for her independence and she wasn't giving it up to the wrong man. If he pushed for too much he'd never get within a hundred feet of either her or Olivia again. Ever.

But he'd have to push her a little or he'd get nowhere either. Only a week ago, he'd thought his life was right where he wanted it, too. Now he knew he was wrong.

He wished they'd met under different circumstances two years ago, and that they'd had a chance to get to know each other before Olivia, because they couldn't really get to know each other right now. Not yet. Not for real. Cass had no idea how awesome he truly was, and what a great father he planned to be. He hoped she would someday soon.

He had to find whoever was selling those classified files as fast as he could. Once his job was done, Cass wasn't pushing him away. He wanted her and Olivia. This was his family.

Right now, she was right. He was getting too close.

He gave a careless shrug of his shoulders. "If anyone complains, remind them I'm a temporary staffer and can do as I please. Besides, I enjoyed spending time with Olivia. And that television in your bedroom is sweet." He reached for his jacket, still hanging on the back of a chair where he'd left it last night. "See you tomorrow morning."

Chapter Nine

Their Monday morning commute was a far more relaxed one than the previous Friday's. Logan didn't feel as angry inside, while Cass didn't seem quite so withdrawn.

And yet there was so much unspoken between them, Logan worried they might never sort it all out.

When they got off the elevator, Cass went straight to her office, her high heels clicking with purpose on the fresh-waxed, shining tiles. She wore a simple navy dress with big gold buttons down the front, looking both sexy and businesslike, and Logan couldn't take his eyes off the sway of her hips as she walked away from him. She fumbled with the key to her door, then was gone.

He fired up the computer at the reception desk.

Less than five minutes later, she was back.

"Did you speak to Maintenance and Security?" she asked.

He looked up from his screen. "Why? Was your door

open again?"

"No. But someone went through the files on my desk. They were spread around, not in a neat pile the way I left them."

That made little sense. No one had any reason to do that. She wouldn't leave classified information sitting on her desk for anyone to steal. She had no access to it to begin with. She'd have to sign the key out, and her name wasn't on the authorized list. Only two people knew where that key was hidden, too, although he was willing to bet it was under someone's desk calendar.

Right next to their computer password.

While there was nothing wrong with Kramer Aerospace's internal procedures for handling government classified material already under contract, by CSIS standards they were seriously outdated. Now that their security system had been breached, when this was over, Kramer Aerospace was going to have to update. Logan already had some recommendations for them to implement. The first was installing a proper security camera.

Until he had the guilty party pegged, however, he didn't dare tip his hand. If he set up his own webcam too soon, and it was noticed, he'd lose his advantage, and no doubt his cover.

"Was it only the files that were touched?" he asked her, slipping right into investigator mode without a second thought.

Cass was too distracted to notice. He could see her running things through in her head. She bit the inside of her lip.

"I'm not really sure," she admitted. "The petty cash is

still there." She fiddled with some papers on the counter above the reception desk, pushing them around with her fingertips, telling him without words how worried she was. "I didn't count it, though."

He pushed away from his computer. "Let's go have another look."

The petty cash was all accounted for. She couldn't find anything missing, only a few other things she was convinced were out of place. When she went through her desk drawers, she insisted that someone had been into them, too.

She folded her arms, the navy fabric of three-quarter-length sleeves pulling back to expose her elbows, and looked as if she were thinking hard.

"I don't get it," she finally said.

He thought he did. He pulled an unlabeled file he'd never seen before from the stack he'd placed on top of her desk on Friday afternoon. Inside it was another folder, this one labeled and in a different color. He recognized right away what it was, and his stomach plunged several levels.

He held it up, the plain side out for her to see, not what was in it. "Where did this come from?"

She spared him an absent glance, her attention elsewhere. "I thought you left me those files so I could do quality inspections on them."

"I did. I must have grabbed this one by mistake." He slipped it from the pile and tucked it under his arm. "I'm going to give Security a call and ask them to change the lock on your door."

He went back to his desk, deeply troubled. He had a problem.

Someone was now actively trying to shift any attention

to Cass. That, in itself, was no big deal. It happened all the time in these types of investigations, and no one with any authority would believe the acting director of the department had left a stolen classified file sitting out on her desk. No one who knew her would ever believe she'd been that careless or stupid.

The problem was that her office door had been left unlocked before he'd started to work in the department, which suggested to him whoever was guilty had anticipated a CSIS investigation.

It was also possible that someone simply didn't like her and wanted to get her demoted or fired. But this seemed more complicated than a simple personal vendetta to him. The information in these classified files was ending up in unfriendly hands. Whoever took it knew what they were doing. If no alarms were raised after a file had been left in her office for her to find, they were going to wonder why not.

You want to make sure that little loophole is closed.

If someone was guilty of espionage, they weren't getting off with a mischief defense.

Since, as an admin assistant, he didn't have authorized access to the classified room, Logan hid the stolen file behind boxes of pens in the supply closet and locked the door. He then pocketed the key.

He'd check with his team to see if the information in that file had ended up somewhere it shouldn't, and to let them know to watch for it if not. After that, he was going to spread office gossip. He'd tell one or two people that he'd somehow picked up a classified file by mistake, and act like he didn't fully grasp the seriousness of such an error.

And he was going to suggest to Baxter Dempsey that

Cass give her staff a lecture about the need for putting files back in their proper places so these kinds of "accidents" never happened again.

• • •

When Baxter came into her office unannounced, shutting the door behind him, Cass knew right away there was trouble. He tugged at the cuffs of his shirtsleeves beneath his suit jacket, a sure sign he had something unpleasant to say.

She liked Baxter. She liked what she saw in his eyes. He was a little shorter than her, with a slight build and a square face, but he was smart and direct. Even so, she knew better than to trust him too much. He liked money and power and didn't bother to pretend otherwise. He'd been generous about helping her navigate through a professional minefield, saving her from critical missteps by guiding her career and handing her opportunities, but she'd known there'd be payback someday. Men like Baxter Dempsey didn't do anything for free.

"We need to talk," Baxter said.

He settled into the visitor's chair across from her. The warm afternoon light shining through the window behind her picked up the worry lines around his eyes.

She pushed aside the report she'd been reading. "What's wrong?"

"I heard a rumor that one of the Department of National Defence's classified files was found, unsecured, on your desk this morning."

At first, she was confused. Then she had an image of Logan pulling a file from the pile, and asking where it came from. Her heart started to pound. "A misplaced file was found. I had no idea it was classified."

Baxter rubbed at his temple, a rueful expression on his face. "That's not exactly helpful. This is your department. How the hell could you not know it was classified?"

Because Logan had whipped it away so fast there'd been no time for her to look at it.

"The folders aren't labeled as classified material," she said. "We don't want to draw attention to them. They're tucked inside a plain folder and marked with a red dot on the inside so the writers know how to handle them when they're working on them." She leaned forward, her palms on her desk. "How on earth did you hear about it?"

"Your temporary admin assistant mentioned it to at least two people. Both of them brought it to my attention."

Cass felt betrayed and conflicted on so many levels, as if Logan should have known better than to talk about something that happened in her office. She'd confided things about her family to him. She'd begun to feel as if she could trust him.

Maybe she was the one who should have known better.

"Speak to your staff about the proper procedures for handling the files," Baxter said. "We'll take a move forward approach with this." He shifted in his chair. "Speaking of moving forward, it's time for the annual performance review of your publications contracts at DND Headquarters in Ottawa."

"I filed all the reports," she said, still reeling from the shock of discovering that a classified file had been left on her desk. Surely any writer working on it would have known better than to give it to the department's admin assistant to place with the regular files for quality inspection. Worse, she couldn't recall any government work authorizations on classified publications. She felt woefully out of the loop, which didn't speak well for her leadership.

"DND insists that you be there for the review."

"Fine," she said, only half listening. "I'll have Logan book a flight. What day?"

He told her. "Better book a hotel room, too. The meetings are scheduled to run for three days, not one."

That got her attention. "I thought we agreed I didn't have to make any overnight trips until Olivia's a little older. I can send one of the supervisors to represent me."

Baxter tapped his leg, a sure sign of growing impatience. "You've been back to work for seven months. You've been acting director for three. I realize you're good at your job, Cass, but you're also young." He held up a hand to stop her from interrupting. "I can't keep giving you preferential treatment. Travel at the customer's request is part of the contract, and they asked specifically for you. They're paying the bill. I'm sorry, but it's nonnegotiable in this particular case." He cleared his throat. Compassion crept into his eyes. "You need to understand a few things. If there's any evidence of mishandling of government information under a contract in a department you run, and Kramer is reprimanded because of it, you'll be held accountable by the company. And you're still under probation in this position. Do you understand what I'm saying?"

She got the message. An ice-cold chill swept through her. Her past performance meant nothing. She'd be fired.

She'd never worried too much about the future, other than the goals she'd set for herself. First, to get out of her father's house. After that, she'd wanted an education and a challenging career.

Now she realized how shortsighted she'd been. How her focus had been too narrow. She had Olivia to think of. How could she pay for a house, a car, and Olivia's future if she were fired?

Baxter rose from his chair. "Speak to your staff about the classified publications."

Cass nodded. She stared at the wall long after Baxter left. He was right when he said she couldn't keep getting preferential treatment. Travel was part of her job description. She'd known she had to plan for this someday. She should have done so by now.

But the thought of being away from Olivia for three whole days, not knowing if she was being loved and well cared for, and unable to reach her in case of an emergency, made her want to put her head between her knees.

She had no babysitter. Patricia often took care of Olivia when meetings ran late or Cass had a dinner appointment, and Cass did the same on the rare occasions when Patricia and her husband were both busy, but this was an imposition and not a reciprocal favor. Plus, that one date with David really had made things awkward—as Logan had warned her it would—since she didn't intend to pursue a relationship.

She had a few friends she trusted, but none of them lived close by. Most were from her college days and had scattered across the country—in some cases, the world. She had no family to fall back on. Her nearest neighbors were wonderful but elderly, and unable to manage an active toddler.

She'd have to ask the daycare for recommendations, which took control out of her hands, and that left her close to hyperventilation again.

Someone knocked on her door. Her head snapped up. "Come in."

The door opened a crack. Logan peered around it, his blue eyes alive with cautious concern. "I'm making a coffee run. Want anything?"

A solution presented itself, one she tried to dismiss. She couldn't ask Logan to babysit again.

But he was also Olivia's father, which was one confidence she felt certain he'd keep. He'd done great with it so far. It wouldn't hurt him to step up and take some responsibility for her, at least until Cass could make more permanent arrangements.

It wouldn't kill her either. When it came to Olivia she discovered she trusted him a lot more than she would any stranger, no matter how highly recommended they might be. She'd simply set boundaries and make sure he respected them.

Besides, she had nowhere else to turn on such short notice.

"Can I speak with you for a minute?" she asked.

• • •

That sounded ominous.

Logan shut the door behind him and took a seat and wondered what Dempsey could have said to Cass to put such fear in her eyes. It was hardly an emotion he'd associate with her. In fact, he'd only ever seen any signs of it in relation to Olivia.

And the lightbulb came on. Her current position was

probationary. Baxter Dempsey had threatened her with termination over that file, possibly in a preemptive strike to cover his own ass, and she couldn't afford to lose this job. Financially, Logan had no doubt she was overextended. She owned a brand-new minivan and an ancient house in bad need of extensive renovations that she'd barely begun. She had a baby to feed.

That was why she looked so completely freaked out right now.

He should have seen this coming, but he'd never had to worry about collateral damage on his end of CSIS investigations before. Had never come face-to-face with its innocent victims. So many people ended up suffering because of the self-serving actions of one single person. He wondered if Dempsey had been the one to plant that file on her desk.

He forced his hands to relax, to lie flat against the brushed-cotton fabric covering his thighs. She didn't know she had no reason to be afraid. Not over money for Olivia. Once the dust settled on this assignment, he was stepping in no matter how things turned out. He wasn't a deadbeat. He owed her months of child support.

He slouched in his chair, rested a foot on one knee, and jiggled his shoe. "What's the problem?"

She spun a pen on her desk, twirling it with her fingers, the skin pinched between her brows. He loved the way the navy dress she wore brought out the gold flecks in the hazel of her eyes. The color suited her. So did the style. She wasn't big into frills, but she was all girl nonetheless.

"I have to go to Ottawa for three days," she said.

That wasn't what he'd expected to hear. Then again, he

had no idea what he'd expected. She wasn't into confidences either, and he wondered where this conversation was heading.

"Stay out of the hotel bars," he replied, only half joking.

She forced a thin smile in response. "What if I need a mojito?"

"I can make you all the mojitos you like, Miss Mary." He smiled. "Name the time and the place."

"I don't need any more mojitos," she said, "but I would like to ask for a favor." The pen spun a little faster. "This trip came up rather suddenly. I've never left Olivia overnight before, and I don't have anyone to babysit. I know I said we shouldn't make a habit of it, but I was wondering if you'd mind."

Her reluctance to ask him was plain, and one part of him wanted to shout *yes* before she could change her mind. The thought of two or three evenings with Olivia, and getting to know her better, was almost too tempting to resist. Having Cass indebted to him also had its own special appeal.

But he'd not only be crossing that line he'd already nudged, he'd be dancing all over it. A few hours here and there were one thing. His ability to carry out an impartial investigation would be compromised by this for sure. Who'd ever believe Cass would ask a man she'd only known for a few weeks to babysit, or that he'd do it out of the goodness of his heart?

He'd have to catch whoever was guilty red-handed in order for any allegations he made against them to stick. If he wasn't careful, someone would walk away over a technicality.

It could even be argued that Logan had left that file on Cass's desk on purpose in order to complicate the investigation if a connection between them, through Olivia, was made. Baxter Dempsey would be certain to bring up that possibility if he thought it would keep Kramer Aerospace out of trouble.

"I don't think it's a good idea," he said.

She set the pen down. She clasped her hands so tight her knuckles whitened. The sunlight behind her caught the warm honey brown of her curls as desperation slithered into her eyes.

"I'll trade you another piece of personal information in exchange," she said. "I promise, I won't expect anything more from you," she added hastily. "Just babysitting, this one time, until I can make more permanent arrangements for the future."

I won't expect anything more from you.

She was going to tell him about Olivia. That he was her father. For a second, he was tempted to let her. It would take so much pressure off him. The decision to remove himself from this assignment would be out of his hands.

But he had the uneasy suspicion that Cass might need someone to protect her — not from the government, but from her own company. To do that, he had to stay right where he was. Her confession would have to wait a while longer.

But he could hardly let her leave Olivia with someone she didn't trust. It would make them both crazy.

"Okay, I'll do it," he said, his reluctance genuine. "But no need to give me any more secrets just yet. The timing's not good for me."

Both her eyebrows went up. "Because you're heading off to tend bar in the Caribbean?"

He'd almost forgotten about that. "All I'm waiting on

right now is the paperwork."

Her lips thinned in a prissy, irritated way that said she didn't believe him. Her eyes narrowed. "I hope you finally picked a country."

Logan stood. He patted the top of her desk and shot her a smile. "Turks and Caicos," he said. "It's Commonwealth, and has the best beaches in the world, not to mention all the five-star restaurants and resorts. You'll have to come for a visit."

Chapter Ten

The timing's not good for me.

All the way home, with Logan stretched out and silent in the passenger seat beside her, his mind clearly elsewhere, Cass wondered what that could possibly mean. For the most part, he was the poster boy for laid-back and relaxed.

Until…he wasn't.

A memory surfaced, one of him naked beneath her in bed. She could recall, in vivid detail, every rigid line, every solid plane, of his body. His dark hair, longer then, contrasted against the bleached starkness of the hotel pillows, creating a shadowy, gray effect like a black-and-white movie still, pierced by the brilliance of the blue in his eyes as he'd smiled up at her.

She'd been in control only because he'd indulged her, and she'd known it. The element of uncertainty about him had made the night that much more exciting for her.

Now it pissed her off because she didn't know what to

believe. She could have sworn he'd been serious about the Caribbean. It had seemed like the perfect path for him to take. She was no longer so sure.

"I'll come over tonight," he said. She pulled her gaze from the road to look at him, momentarily confused. "So you can give me the rundown on Olivia's schedule," he added, heat in his gaze as if he knew what she'd been thinking about, and her entire body flushed.

She turned into her driveway and shut off the engine. It ticked in the sudden silence. Neither one of them made a move to get out.

"Aren't you picking up Olivia from daycare?" he asked.

"Not in the van. We usually walk unless it's raining. She likes the fresh air." So did Cass. She spent the day cooped up in an office.

"I'm coming with you." He had his door open and one foot on the ground, but Cass still hadn't moved, so he paused with a question on his face as if wondering what was holding her up. "You'll want to introduce me to the staff so they know I'll be standing in for you for a few days, right?"

"Of course. Right." She gave herself a hard mental shake. The daycare wouldn't release Olivia to anyone without her permission.

She got out, and with a press of the button on her key fob, locked her briefcase and purse in the minivan.

The walk was pleasant and warm. The sun shone through the trees. Birds sang from between the fresh new leaves of branches that draped over the sidewalk, creating a latticework canopy.

When they weren't in the office, or she didn't have driving or Olivia to focus her attention on, Cass couldn't deny she felt more than a smidgeon of physical attraction for Logan. He might give the appearance of any professional at the end of a long day, jacketless and tieless, but wearing a pale gray cotton dress shirt with rolled-up cuffs and well-pressed black trousers, he looked better than most. The dove gray of his shirt brought out the blue of his eyes.

He matched his stride to hers because she was hampered by her high heels. One caught in a crack in the sidewalk, and he shot out a hand to steady her. His fingers curled around her elbow, firm and warm through the fabric of her sleeve.

Rather than release her, he took hold of her hand and tucked it into the fold of his arm. Then he settled his hand over hers so she couldn't withdraw it. The gentlemanly gesture charmed her, mostly because he had no reason to make one. He had nothing to prove. Nothing to gain.

Nothing he really wanted.

"Why do you always wear such impractical shoes?" he asked. "I mean, I like them. But they seem as if they'd be hard to walk in. And you're already tall, so you must have a reason."

"When I'm dealing with men, especially ones used to giving orders, I find they take me more seriously if they have to look up to me," she said. "Ridiculous, but true."

The pads of his fingertips stroked against hers in a decidedly ungentleman-like manner that made her stomach flutter. "I don't think it's ridiculous at all. In fact, I think we've established that I like looking up to you."

Since he was taller than she was, even when she wore heels, she got the inference. She also knew she should ignore him when he said things like that, but she couldn't seem to resist. What he lacked in some areas he more than made up for in others. He had a good sense of humor, quiet but quick.

"You were looking up *at* me, not *to* me," she said. "There's a difference."

His lips twitched with amusement. "Not if your intention was to make me take you seriously, because I most definitely did."

"Is that why you call me Miss Mary?" she asked. "Because you take me so seriously?"

He came to an abrupt halt, forcing her to stop, too. They were two doors away from the daycare, where parents and children were coming and going. Three cars were parked along the sidewalk, two of them running. The Mazda to her immediate right was empty.

He lowered his voice. Heat crept into his eyes. "I call you Miss Mary because it means I want to take you. And I'm very serious about that."

He didn't give her a chance to reply, or gather her thoughts, which were now in complete disarray. He began walking again, faster now, forcing her to half run in her heels in order to keep pace. She arrived at the daycare out of breath and befuddled, unable to think.

Logan took charge.

He introduced himself to the two women on duty, explaining that Cass would be away at the first of next week, and he'd be picking up Olivia for three days. He wrote down his name and his cellphone number for them. He didn't say who he was in relation to either Cass or Olivia. He let them think what they liked.

And Cass knew what they thought. One look at Olivia in Logan's arms after she'd toddled over to him, insisting he pick her up, said it all.

She'd assumed he would be more discreet.

"You did that on purpose," she accused him once Olivia had been settled in her stroller and they were out on the street, headed for home.

"Did what?" he asked. He'd taken command of the stroller, too, leaving Cass to scurry along beside them in her impractical heels.

"Made them think…" Her voice trailed off and she bit her lip, changing her mind regarding what she'd been about to blurt out.

She couldn't figure him out. What his game was.

"Made them think what, Cass?" His steps slowed. He turned his head to look at her. "That maybe I'm Olivia's father?"

Her breath hiccupped in her chest, its rhythm interrupted by a curious mixture of fear and relief. She wasn't ready for this, after all.

She didn't trust him enough.

Then he shrugged a shoulder and turned back to the stroller, maneuvering it over the bumps and cracks in the sidewalk like a pro. "So what if they do? I'm sure her real father wouldn't have a problem with anyone thinking it."

"Maybe I have a problem," she said. "I like my personal life private."

His steps slowed again. "I see."

"I'm not so sure you do." She took a deep breath. "I have to live here. I have to care what people think. The things I do reflect on Olivia. It's the same way at work." She sneaked a peek at his face, which showed nothing of what he was thinking. "I need this job. I'd rather my staff didn't know that my administrative assistant is babysitting for me."

"Private, huh?" His gaze on her was hotter than she was expecting. His lips curved into a smile that didn't bode well. Not for keeping any distance between them. "Not to worry, Miss Mary. I can do private."

That was the biggest problem, Cass thought, far from reassured. He did private too well.

• • •

It sucked more than a little to have Cass pulling rank. As soon as she returned from her trip, Logan was telling his team about Olivia.

The daycare had made fatherhood real. Perhaps it was the level of responsibility involved. Or the way Olivia had greeted him, with a single-toothed, drooly smile, as if he were the most important person in her world and she wanted everyone to know it. His daughter deserved a daddy as much as any other child, and it was going to be him.

A huge weight he hadn't realized he'd been carrying seemed to fall from his shoulders. He'd ask to be kept on the case since he was already in. He'd explain to the team leader why he believed Cass couldn't be guilty, and make sure they had access to all the information he had on her. That included her family history, although the thought of giving it up made him feel like the worst kind of snitch. Cass's issues over privacy centered around trust.

He took a last sip of water as he finished his dinner, trying not to rush. His grandmother always prepared him a hot meal at night despite him telling her it wasn't necessary, and insisted they eat at the dining room table, because she liked the routine and the formality. He saw no reason not to indulge her.

"What are your plans for the rest of the evening?" his grandmother asked.

He laid his napkin beside his plate, smoothing it flat with his palm, and thought about how much he should say. At some point he was going to have to tell her that he'd be staying with Olivia while Cass was away, and she'd wonder why. If he told her too much too soon, she might let something slip. If he didn't tell her enough, she'd be hurt when the truth about Olivia finally came out.

No matter what, or when, explaining the situation with Cass and Olivia to his grandmother was going to prove awkward.

"Cass has a business trip next week, and she had no one to take care of Olivia. She was panicked about it, so I offered to help out. I'm going over to her place this evening so she can give me the rundown on Olivia's routine."

His grandmother said nothing for a moment. The flickering candlelight caught the glittering gray threads in her hair, now streaked with white, an abrupt reminder to him that she wasn't getting any younger. Much of the sparkle in her eyes he remembered from when he was a boy had dimmed, too. Her mind hadn't dulled however, despite the tendency she sometimes had of allowing her conversation to meander. She always came back to the point she intended to make.

She folded her hands in her lap and gazed steadily at him across the gleaming mahogany table. "I don't know what Cass's story is, but I do know that she desperately wants stability in Olivia's life, and she's worked hard to get it. No matter what the reason is for you taking a job in her office, and whether your interest in her is personal or professional, I hope you aren't going to ruin that much for her, at least. Please don't hurt her."

"My interest is personal," he said. "And I don't plan to hurt her."

His grandmother relaxed. Much of the stiffness went out of her shoulders. Still, she looked doubtful. "Cass is lonely. She has no one she can count on, and she doesn't trust easily. She needs someone who'll be there for her. The fact that she's had to ask someone who's almost a stranger to take care of Olivia says a lot. For some reason she trusts you, and as much as I love you, I'm not sure she should. You don't live a very stable life, Logan. You never stay in one place for more than a few months. You disappear without notice. You keep secrets from everyone. That's no kind of life for a young family. It's certainly not a good one for Cass and Olivia."

He'd never told his grandmother what he did for a living. It wasn't something he was free to discuss. She'd known he had a job with the government, but no one he knew outside of work could say for certain that he was with CSIS. And while he wished he could come right out and discuss this with her, if he could, a discussion would have to take place between him and Cass first.

"You're getting a bit ahead of things, Nan. I agreed to take care of Olivia for a few days."

"Then, if it's personal, as you say, are you really interested in Cass?" His grandmother placed her palm on the table, drumming her fingers as if making a point. "Or is it Olivia?"

He kept his face still, not daring to give anything away. He could think of no response that wouldn't get him into trouble a few weeks down the road. He started to sweat, the heat building at the back of his collar before spreading under his shirt like an inverted volcanic eruption.

His grandmother had missed her calling in life. She should have taken up interrogation. Instead, she'd been a librarian.

"I don't need an answer," she said. "I want you to think. With your head. Cass would never leave Olivia with a stranger, especially a man, if she didn't have a good reason to think it was safe. Whatever you've done, Logan, I expect you to fix this. You're a grown man. Take some responsibility."

It was interesting to hear his grandmother's conclusions about Cass, which weren't so very different from the ones he'd already drawn. On the surface she seemed capable and well-adjusted, but the first time he'd met her, he'd pegged her as someone with daddy issues. Turned out, he'd been right. He couldn't forget the look on her face when she told him she'd been thrown out of her father's house. She'd been too calm and matter-of-fact.

He wondered how deep her scars ran that his grandmother felt so protective of her. He already knew she had trust issues, and he'd told her a lot of untruths, but he wasn't the only one keeping secrets. He'd been cut out of his daughter's life. He didn't like that he'd been turned into the bad guy when he felt more like the victim.

He *wanted* to fix this, more than anyone could imagine.

"Don't hurt her," his grandmother repeated as he excused himself from the table.

Chapter Eleven

"I've changed my mind," Logan announced when he walked through Cass's door.

His dark hair was wet from the rain that battered the side of the house and sluiced down its windows. Water had beaded on the oilskin surface of his weatherproof jacket, and it dripped to the floor as he shrugged the jacket off. Underneath the jacket, he wore a long-sleeved, blue-and-white jersey and jeans.

Olivia was already tucked in bed. Cass was folding laundry at the kitchen table—tiny T-shirts and leggings that she then stacked into neat little piles.

Her heart lurched, thinking he meant he was no longer willing to look after Olivia, until he continued.

"I do want to buy one more secret off you. But I get to choose it."

She folded the last frilly pink T-shirt into a tidy square and laid it on top of its companions, concentrating on the task, not wanting him to see how rattled she was. Or relieved.

Since she'd known he was coming over she'd opted for sneakers instead of bunny slippers, and pale gray yoga pants rather than her usual baggy sweats. The evening was damp and chilly, so she'd pulled on a warm, cream-colored, cable-knit sweater. She'd also left her hair loose because he seemed to like it that way best.

He frustrated and confused her. He made her feel both comfortable and afraid. She wanted to throw him off balance, to unsettle him as much as he unsettled her, and this attraction between them was the only way she could think of to do it, the only position of power she had with him. But it was double-edged.

"Fair enough. But I get to decide whether or not I want to sell it to you," she said.

He caught hold of a chair, swung it around, and straddled it so that he faced her. He rested his folded arms along its back, between the spindles, and settled his chin on one wrist. His eyes ran over her in a way that said he did, indeed, like what he saw, and warmed her in places she'd do well to ignore.

Which meant she'd only really succeeded in unsettling herself.

He smiled at her, a gentle prompt in his eyes. "You were going to go over Olivia's routine with me?"

She flushed when she realized she'd been silent too long, watching him in the same way he stared at her.

"I've written it all down." She reached for the spreadsheet she'd stuck to the fridge door and pulled it free of the magnet that held it in place.

His smile spread, deepening the creases that bracketed

his lips. "Of course you have."

She paused, the spreadsheet in her hand. This, she could deal with. Her eyebrows lifted in challenge. "Are you suggesting I'm a control freak, Mr. Alexander?"

"No. I'm stating it flat-out, Miss Mary," he drawled. "You've written me an instruction manual, not a schedule."

She examined the three-page spreadsheet she held. "I can see why you might think that, but I consider it more of a reference document. I prefer to preempt hearing 'That's not in my job description.' This provides clarity and will preclude any arguments over my expectations."

"Let me see it." He took the spreadsheet from her and read the first item out loud. "'5:00 p.m. Pick up Olivia from daycare (no later than 5:20 p.m.).' I can understand why it's important to write that one down. I might be so anxious to start watching your flat-screen TV straight after work that I forget her existence. I'm not as sure it's necessary to remind me to hang her jacket in the closet by the front door."

"I like to cover my bases," she said. "It leaves no room for error."

He looked up from his reading. "You've included a menu."

"She's a baby. She can't eat burgers and fries or frozen pizza."

"Which shows how little you know me. When was the last time you saw me eat a burger or fries? What did I have for lunch today at the office?"

Cass tried to think. She'd only ever seen him eat birthday cake and French toast, and only then because she'd served them to him. She frowned. "You aren't vegan, are you? Or kosher?"

The corners of his mouth twitched again as he scratched a thumb along his jaw. "No. Let's just agree that I know better than to feed Olivia junk food."

She tapped the spreadsheet in triumph. "I've taken that worry away. Everything's precooked, labeled, and stacked in the freezer."

He stretched out an arm and dropped the papers on the table. He rose from the chair, sliding it neatly back into place so it lined up with the others. "You're a complex woman, Cass. I'll give you that. It makes me more worried about you going off to Ottawa on business for three days than I ought to be."

The baby monitor sitting on the counter emitted a soft sniffle and a sigh as Olivia rolled over in her sleep. The refrigerator kicked in a second later, the motor humming.

He was standing too close to her, and without her heels on, she found herself staring straight at his chin. A faint hint of shadow stained his smooth skin. She wasn't a lot shorter than he was, but enough that she'd have to look up, and no way was she doing that. Not after her telling him why she wore heels to work.

"I don't know what you're talking about," she said to his throat.

"You're Dr. Jekyll and Mrs. Hyde. One part of you, the part you let people see, is very organized and self-contained. One might say driven. But once you're out of the spotlight…" She waited, ready to argue his take on her personality, but he plunged his hands into his back pockets and changed the subject. "Show me where you keep the diapers and towels and anything else I might need, and where you want me to sleep."

She led him upstairs, very aware of his presence behind her, and each step of the way, a tiny alarm bell jingled in the back of her head. In the past she'd always heeded that warning, but with Logan, Olivia was all the warning she needed.

She liked him too much. She didn't trust him at all.

Maybe he was right about her having two sides. Right now, the practical side dared the other to prove she could resist him.

She showed him the linen closet where she kept the diapers, as well as the extra sheets and blankets for Olivia's crib, then started down the long hall toward her bedroom. He'd have to sleep there. The two unused bedrooms were empty and in need of repairs.

He stopped at the partially opened door to Olivia's room. Inside it was dark, but the light from the hall was enough to illuminate her tiny form in the center of her pink-and-white crib. She'd rolled to her stomach again and hiked up her knees so that her diaper-clad, pink-pajama-covered bottom stuck up in the air. She'd crawled from under the blankets, and the night was cool.

Before Cass could make a move, he tiptoed in and tucked them around Olivia again. He captured one of her dark, glossy curls between his thumb and two fingers, rubbing it as he stared down at her with an expression of abject adoration and longing on his face.

He'd claimed that Cass was complex, but he was a fine one to talk. He was clearly already in love with his daughter and yet refused to do anything about it.

Cass had seen enough. She crooked a finger into the waist of his jeans and gave a sharp tug. He followed her back into the hall and then into her bedroom, where she shut the door with a firm *click* of the latch. Then she rounded on him, prepared to confront this, once and for all.

Even though it scared her to death.

He cut her off before she could begin.

"I'm ready to collect on that secret you owe me. I want to know what happened with your father. What *really* happened," he said.

Her mind went blank, stripping as it tried to shift gears. "*That's* the secret you want from me?"

"Yes." He was quietly emphatic. "I want to know when you first ran away from home. I want to know why. And I want to know why you went back if you were so anxious to leave, and when your father just as obviously didn't want you there."

She perched on the edge of the bed, all the wind gone from her sails, and tried to figure out where this new game of his was leading. That question was, without a doubt, the least important one he could have asked of her, and so far from her thoughts she had no idea where to begin.

He should have asked about Olivia. It was as if he really didn't want to know.

He didn't join her on the bed. Instead, he leaned against the closed door as if to block her escape.

"It's no deep, dark secret," Cass said. "I was four when I ran away the first time. He spanked me for something I didn't do. I hit him back, and he spanked me again. I was angry because he wouldn't let me explain."

"That's why you like to be taller than men," he said. "You found out the hard way that bigger is better."

She rolled her eyes at him. "Don't read too much into it,

Dr. Freud. I was four. Everyone was bigger than me, and it was a spanking, not a beating. *That* was when I discovered it's important to plan an escape. I got as far as the highway before one of the neighbors picked me up and took me home."

"They never asked why you ran away?"

"They didn't need to." She tucked her hands between her knees. "My father's a coldhearted, uncompromising man, Logan. It's hard to hide that from your neighbors in a small community. He thinks bullying and intimidation pass for discipline, but he never crossed the line into physical abuse. They had no reason not to mind their own business."

"Mental cruelty is another form of abuse," Logan said. His face had gone hard.

His defense warmed her. She'd never had anyone take her side growing up, which was one reason she loved Mrs. Sheridan and her friends. They were nosy and kind.

But she didn't like anyone, especially not Logan, thinking her weak.

"I could take it," she said. "My mother and sisters, not so much. They chose to do things his way. I saved my money for years, then ran away again at fifteen. I hitchhiked halfway across the country and had the time of my life until I ran out of money. When I applied for work at a restaurant and the owner figured out I was too young for the job, she called Social Services on me. It was the social worker who pointed out that if I really wanted to escape, education was the best road to freedom. She helped me make a real plan. I spent the next three years studying hard."

"He didn't give you any credit for that either, I bet."

She wanted to be fair to her father. In her own way, she

was every bit as stubborn. She got it from him.

"I wasn't blameless. I made time for fun. I was as wild as my father said, and I knew what buttons to push. But I never did anything illegal. Ever. Except maybe underage drinking." She cracked a thin smile. "The point is, I worked to meet my expectations, not his. When I told him I'd won scholarships to university and planned to be an engineer, rather than be happy for me, and proud, he told me no daughter of his was taking a job away from a man. Since I wouldn't go into nursing or teaching instead, or something he thought more feminine, he said to get out and never come back. I was happy to go."

"He's never tried to contact you since then? Never seen how well you've turned out?"

She had to laugh. "Are you even listening?" she asked. "By his standards, I haven't. But because I have a mother and sisters who I thought might care, I did write to them after Olivia was born. I got a note back from my father telling me to stay away from them all. He called her a bastard." She shrugged. "They know where to find me if they want to see me. Or Olivia."

"Your father's an ass," Logan said.

"He can't change who he is." She'd accepted that a long time ago. "More importantly, he doesn't want to. I don't want to change either, so I can hardly criticize him for it, but I do blame him for his reaction to Olivia. He's the real bastard in the family."

As she waited to hear what Logan said next, she decided he'd asked her the right question after all. She was glad she hadn't insisted on discussing Olivia with him, because telling him about her past reminded her that it wasn't possible to force people to do things they didn't want or be someone they couldn't. She wasn't going to ask him to live up to her expectations. Sooner or later he'd come to hate her.

Olivia would be fine without him.

But she wondered if he would be fine without Olivia. She didn't believe she'd mistaken his irritation with her earlier, at the daycare, or misconstrued his words. *Made them think what, Cass? That maybe I'm Olivia's father?*

He seemed so conflicted about it. Or at least, that was the impression she got. Maybe three days with Olivia would help him to make up his mind about what part, if any, he wanted to play in her life.

Then maybe Cass could figure out how they could move forward.

...

Logan couldn't take his eyes off Cass. She looked so pretty, and fresh, with all those untidy ringlets, that bulky knit sweater, and her clingy gray pants. So very different from the self-assured woman he'd met in Ottawa, and knew at the office.

Or the fearless, fifteen-year-old girl who'd somehow survived hitchhiking across half the country.

Which proved once again how deceiving appearances could be. He'd read her right, but also wrong. He'd wondered how her relationship with her father might have affected her, and worried about it, but as it turned out, if anything her issues with him had made her stronger. She really was capable and well-adjusted, if maybe a touch too uncompromising. If Olivia had inherited even half of her mother's strength of will, then he didn't doubt they would have their hands full in a few years.

Personally, he liked strong women. And the more he learned about Cass, the more he liked her in particular. He'd had a few serious relationships in the past, but they'd always ended in him walking away. His work meant he had to be secretive about a lot of his actions, and most of the women he'd met had difficulty dealing with that.

Cass was different.

Special.

If she walked away, she'd never look back.

The possibility filled him with panic. He couldn't allow that to happen. Soon, everything was going to be out in the open and they could start over.

She was waiting for him to speak. He knew enough about her by now to be careful not to utter meaningless platitudes unless he meant to be funny. While she didn't live in the past, she'd learned to be unforgiving. And she hated to be analyzed.

He sent up a prayer to the diplomacy gods.

"Did you bring me in here to watch television?" he asked. "Or for some other reason?"

He saw the relief creeping into her eyes. It mirrored his own that he'd read her right.

A dimple flashed in her cheek. "Some other reason. This is where you'll be sleeping while I'm away. It's also got the bathroom Olivia and I use."

He'd already figured that out after having spent one night here before. He let her show him everything anyway—the towels, the baby soap, powder, and shampoo—because she needed that level of control. Leaving Olivia for a few days was going to be difficult for her.

It was a good-sized room, with a claw-foot tub beneath the window backed by white wainscoting. Inside the tub was a basket of toys, wet from Olivia's bath. A glass shower enclosure filled a corner. A row of shelves held towels and what looked like a hundred items of makeup, lotions, and perfumes. A change table stood beside the toilet. On the other side of the toilet was a vanity and sink. Everything was shining and new. Organized. And white, with pink accents.

He'd love to know what went on inside that Jekyll-and-Hyde, engineer's brain of hers.

"What—no list?" he inquired.

She swung the door closed. On the inside, she'd taped Olivia's morning and evening bathroom routines.

"Huh." He'd known it would be there. He enjoyed baiting her. She knew what he was doing, too, and yet she couldn't seem to stop herself from reacting to it.

Or to him.

He enjoyed that most of all.

They were only a few feet apart. He reached for her hand and pulled her toward him, not saying anything, uncertain of what she might do if he kissed her, but deciding he'd take his chances.

She surprised him again by stepping into his arms and burying her face against him. "I don't want to go on this trip."

Any desire he had to tease her ended right there. She was looking for comfort and had turned to him. He couldn't begin to describe how great it made him feel.

"I know you don't," he said, murmuring into her soft mass of hair as he cradled her closer. "But I swear to you, I will follow your lists to the very last detail. I won't feed

Olivia pizza. She will never know that you're gone. She'll just think you got taller and turned incredibly handsome."

She laughed into his chest, her shoulders shaking, her words muffled. "I don't suppose you'd consider taking on a new job as a nanny?"

"Live-in?" he asked. "I'm not so sure. My grandmother's right next door. She might not approve of the arrangement. Or are we talking about another role-playing game?" He burrowed his chin between her shoulder and neck and whispered into her ear. "Because she wouldn't need to know about that."

That made her laugh harder. Her grip on him tightened in a halfhearted hug, and then it relaxed, although she didn't let go. "Thank you. For understanding," she added, as if he might not be able to figure that out.

He could see her, tall and slender in his arms, her curls spilling over his hands, glowing in the fierce light of the vanity mirror. He remembered how she'd felt when he'd held her their one night together, all smooth-skinned and firm and soft where a woman should be.

He ran his palms over the back of her sweater, easing them under her arms and up her sides until he cupped her face between his hands. He stroked his thumbs along the lines of her jaw, his fingers tracing her cheekbones, mapping the delicate structure beneath her skin. Her eyes fixed onto his, darkening as the laughter in them faded away.

At some point, he wasn't sure when, Cass had taken on a new meaning for him. He was past the anger. Most of it, at any rate. She wasn't simply some woman he'd picked up in a bar. She was also more than the mother of his child. She was a woman he wanted more than his next breath. While he was terrified by the thought of losing Olivia, he was equally afraid of losing Cass. He wanted them both.

"I couldn't believe my good luck when you came back to the bar," he confessed. His voice sounded hoarse, grinding out past the lump in his throat. "You're even more beautiful now than you were when I met you."

She wasn't all that impressed by his honesty. "You liked that I was only interested in hooking up for one night."

"True. But I wouldn't have said no to a second." He pressed a kiss to her lips, then another for emphasis, and tossed the ball back to her. "I wouldn't say no to one now, either."

He expected her to laugh again, or maybe retreat into her private thoughts, but she didn't. She gazed at him steadily, her lovely face serious. "What would be the point?"

He kissed the underside of her jaw, scraping the stubble on his chin lightly along her soft skin and sucked in the scent of baby soap and vanilla. "It's obvious that you're ready to start meeting men again, and we already know that we're good together. You're a beautiful woman, Cass. Life has to be lonely for you with only a baby and a few elderly neighbors to keep you company. That's no way to live." He didn't bring up that she'd gone out with the brother of a friend, or mention that he'd snooped through her tablet and knew she'd been looking at online-dating sites. "What's holding you back? Are you worried about the fact that technically, you're my boss?"

"It's my daughter I'm worried about. I don't want people flitting in and out of her life."

His grandmother had said much the same thing to him, and he guessed now he got it. He wanted so much to be able to come right out and say that he wouldn't be leaving this time, because he wasn't. Not permanently. Only for work. He'd make Nova Scotia his home base, because Olivia was going to know her real father.

He wanted Cass to know the real Logan, too. He'd never hurt her, no matter what his grandmother thought. Together, they'd make this work. But if they were going to have a "knockdown, drag 'em out fight" over this, it could wait until she got back.

So, instead of the meaningful things he'd rather be saying to her, he made himself sound like the loser she'd pegged him as.

"You're thinking too much."

"I haven't been thinking enough." She shrugged out of his arms. Regret spilled from her eyes. "I'm not over Olivia's father. I thought I was, but I'm not."

He had no idea what to make of that. It sounded both promising, and not.

"Maybe you should give the guy a second chance," he said. "And some time to adjust. I'm sure Olivia came as a surprise to him. Not an unwelcome one," he added hastily. "Maybe just not at a good time."

Again, he knew that made him sound like a loser. Finding out she was pregnant and alone couldn't have come at a good time for her either. He wanted to make that up to her as soon as he could. To Olivia, too.

"I'm not sure I can trust him," Cass said. "He's not what he seems."

Logan wasn't going there. "I'm sure he's exactly what he seems. All you need to do is look for the right things."

A frown formed a delicate vee between her brows. "I'm

not looking for anything but honesty."

He had no answer for that, so he kept his mouth shut.

She chewed on her bottom lip. Then she stepped in close, locked her fingers in the front of his shirt, and kissed him, a light peck on the lips.

"One more chance," she said, and Logan's heart started an enthusiastic victory dance. She patted his chest and met his eyes. "But he'd better not blow it. I don't plan on sleeping with a stranger ever again."

He heard the warning in her words, and saw it in her eyes, but there was no danger of that. She knew him better than anyone. She didn't know yet that she did, but she'd find out soon enough.

He settled a palm on the line of her spine, tracing the length of it to the small of her back. He pressed her against him, trapping her elbows, holding her so that their lower bodies melded from hip to knee. He bent his head and kissed her.

Really kissed her. For the first time in two years. The months between then and now slipped away.

She inched her arms upward between them so that she cupped his face in her hands, and she parted her lips, flicking her tongue against his. Heat lanced under his ribs, diving straight to his groin. His fingers caught at the bottom of her sweater, meeting smooth, warm flesh. She held her breath, then sighed against his lips, arching against him.

The sweater came off. He caught a glimpse of her naked back, already braless, in the mirror behind her as he dropped it onto the floor. He rubbed his thumb along the delicate underside of one breast, cupping its weight.

Her arms had snaked around his neck, and she pressed

her mouth against the side of his throat, tickling his skin with the tip of her tongue.

"Shirt," she murmured into his ear. "Now."

He let her go long enough to oblige, jerking it over his head and letting it fall to the bathroom floor with her sweater. He swept her off her feet and into his arms and she gasped, clutching him tight for a second. Then, she reached behind him for the bathroom door to swing it out of the way so he could carry her through to the bedroom. She laughed as he tossed her onto the enormous bed, and threw her arms above her head, her mass of light brown curls tangled around her. She looked lovely, all half-naked and so sensual that his throat went dry. It felt as if it had been buffed with fine sandpaper.

He hooked the waistband of her pants in his fingers and slowly tugged them over her hips, peeling them off her thighs and those long, slender calves he'd been admiring for days.

The laughter died on her lips. She rolled to her knees and reached for him where he stood at the side of her bed. She snagged her fingers in his belt loops and kissed him.

She caught his lower lip between her teeth, taking him by surprise so that he couldn't make any sudden moves. She eased the button of his jeans free before sliding the zipper down, inch by excruciating inch, the rasping sound of metal on metal loud in the quiet room.

"Take them off," she said, heat in her eyes.

He sucked air into his lungs, amused and very aroused. He enjoyed the way she gave orders. But if Miss Mary thought she was taking the driver's seat this time, she was sadly mistaken.

Tonight was about building a level of trust. Of staking a

claim. Letting her know his intentions.

He took a step back. He lifted a brow. His voice came out husky, as if he'd been running. Hard.

"If you want them," he said, "come and get them."

He studied her face as she considered the challenge he'd extended. He wondered how much she wanted him. How badly. She ran her gaze from the bulge at the open flaps of his jeans, up his stomach and chest, all the way to his eyes.

Then she smiled, wide-eyed with fake innocence. "Shall I also turn down zee sheets *pour vous, monsieur*?"

A French maid. It took everything he had not to laugh. This round went to Cass.

Logan, however, didn't want to play games. At least, not tonight. He had too much at stake to be anything less than serious about this. "I think I'll turn down my own sheets this time."

He shucked out of his jeans, kicked them aside, then stalked toward the bed, fully naked and already erect. Laughing, Cass fell backward. He sprawled out beside her, throwing one leg across hers and pinning her down.

He liked making her laugh. More than that, he liked tugging those soft little sighs from her that he remembered she made at all the right moments.

There was one little problem. His pockets were empty.

"Condoms?" he asked.

"I'm on the pill," she replied. Her eyes never left his face. "I learned my lesson the last time."

He shifted to his side and reached across her to slide his palm from the underside of her arm, through the dip of valley at her waist, and up the rise to her hip. Her skin was soft and smooth, and when he kissed her bare shoulder, she tasted fresh, like the spring air outside. He leaned over and took one of her breasts in his mouth, rolling the taut tip between his teeth as he teased it with his tongue. She moaned.

Satisfaction warred with desire. The small sound was like fuel to a fire. He slid his hand between her thighs, tracing his fingers through the soft, warm folds of her flesh.

"Please, Logan," she whispered, her voice husky with want.

That was about as much self-control as he figured any man could handle. He'd dreamed about her for months. The reality was so, so much better.

He lifted himself onto his hands, gazing down at her face, as he nudged her thighs apart with one knee. She had her hands on his hips, staring at his mouth with hunger in her eyes.

He kissed her. As he did, he positioned himself so that, with one slow, gentle thrust, he was inside her. She sighed, closing her eyes, and rocked her hips against him until he couldn't breathe. He didn't move but stayed as he was, enjoying the pleasure on her face, and the impatience she didn't bother trying to hide.

His arms were shaking, he discovered.

She wrapped her legs around the backs of his, bringing him deeper, and he took several long breaths. Then, he drew back until he'd almost completely withdrawn, and thrust again, slow and deep. He did it again, over and over, until she was breathless, too, and her soft sighs turned to low, needy cries.

She stiffened, arched her back, and with a moan of pure pleasure, he felt her muscles clench around him. He buried his own cries against her throat as his orgasm erupted in response to hers.

When the bedroom stopped spinning, he shifted his weight to the side, easing Cass along with him so that she was on top. He wrapped his arms around her. Her body was limp, and she sighed with contentment as she nestled against him. He felt her heart beating against his chest, a hard, fast rhythm at first, that gentled, then slowed. He pressed his cheek into her hair.

He was in love with her.

The discovery alarmed him more than fatherhood had, because he'd been lying to her since the very beginning and he had no idea how she'd react when she found out.

He was keeping secrets from his bosses now, too. But only until Cass got back from her business trip.

This wasn't a complication, he told himself. This was right where he needed to be. He could keep everything separate. She wanted privacy. He'd give her as much as he could. Being a part of Cass's and Olivia's lives had become as important to him as his job.

In fact, a lot more.

Chapter Twelve

Logan drove Cass to the airport early on the morning of her flight, before taking Olivia to day care, where he'd been grilled by one of the other mothers.

Cass's friend Patricia certainly was nosy, although he conceded that her protectiveness was nice. She genuinely liked Cass.

He should have known that his growing relationship with Cass would spill over into their everyday lives. As a result of the interrogation, he'd arrived at work a half an hour late, which raised a few eyebrows. Not to mention he was driving her minivan.

He hung up his jacket and went to start his computer, his finger on the button, when he noticed something wasn't quite right. A few things were out of place on his desk—more than could be attributed to the cleaners, who wiped down bare surfaces and didn't touch anything else. The angle of his keyboard was also off.

The webcam he'd bought and installed a few days ago was missing. When he checked, so was the program that stored the images it recorded.

To make things more interesting, someone had logged on to his computer using Cass's ID. He knew she couldn't possibly have done so.

He stared at the screen, possibilities swirling in his head. Without a doubt, someone was sending him a message. A bold one, at that.

He thought it all through. The original thefts hadn't been carefully hidden. Cass's office was sloppily and meaninglessly searched. A file had been left on her desk, begging to be discovered. Now, whoever was behind all of it had targeted him.

Using Cass's information.

While this had a mischief defense written all over it, it also had something a little bit more.

He got up and went to the lunchroom. One of the writers was sitting at a table, sipping his coffee and reading a newspaper.

Ivan, the surly former Griffon pilot.

He walked to the coffeepot and poured himself a mugful. He slammed the pot back on the burner with calculated force.

Ivan looked up from his paper. "What's got your knickers in a knot? Lose your nail file?"

Cute.

"My webcam," he replied, pulling a chair up to the table so he was sitting across from the writer. "Someone stole it off my monitor, and even took the time to wipe the program clean. Bastard."

The only emotion Ivan gave off was one of complete boredom. "Why did you have a webcam hooked up in the first place?"

"The last job I had, someone swiped office supplies, and I took the blame. Not for stealing them. For not keeping them more secure. I'm not making that mistake again. I didn't think anyone would notice the camera."

"Good luck filing a complaint." Ivan went back to reading his paper. "It's against company policy to bring in personal equipment. I hear it's a hanging offense."

"Thanks. You've been a big help."

Logan took his coffee and returned to work. It wouldn't be long before that rumor spread, no matter how indifferent Ivan pretended to be. It was too good not to share.

When morning break time arrived, Isabelle sauntered up to his desk. "I hear you lost a webcam. If you're so worried about the office supplies, I could hang onto the key for you. I have plenty of good hiding places."

"What is it with you and the office supplies?" he asked. "Don't you get paid enough?"

Isabelle laughed. It ended on a raspy smoker's cough. "They're part of the benefit package. We all do our school shopping here. I've got a six-year-old grandson to care for."

"He goes through a lot of sticky notes and pens for a six-year-old. Want me to order some coloring books and crayons instead?"

"Give it a year or two until Cass's little girl is old enough to color, and maybe then she'll sign off on that order. But by then, Nathan will be too old for coloring books. He'll want the sticky notes more, so I see them as an investment in his future."

Logan had a good memory for detail and something about her having a grandson seemed odd to him. Then he had it. Her personnel file showed no next of kin, yet for her to have a grandchild there must be a son or a daughter somewhere.

And she didn't like Cass. To him, that was a gigantic red flag. Cass hadn't done anything to earn her dislike.

"You don't look old enough to be a grandmother," he said.

Isabelle's face closed over, and he knew he'd pushed a button.

"I had my son while I was in high school." She glanced at her watch and shifted the subject. "I'm running out for a muffin. Can I get you anything?"

He ordered one, too. When she was gone he took the stairs to the sixth floor and ducked into an empty conference room. He dug his cell phone from his pocket and dialed one of his team members. He asked that they do some digging on Isabelle Walsh and for her to be placed under twenty-four-hour surveillance.

Later that afternoon, shortly before the end of the day, Logan's office phone rang. He knew who it would be.

"Hey, Cass," he said. "How are the meetings?"

"Boring."

There was a bit of a pause and he grinned into the receiver. He turned away from the reception area so he could carry on the conversation in semiprivacy. He was going to make her come right out and say why she'd called.

"Don't forget to pick up Olivia," she finally said.

He leaned back in his chair and propped one foot on the corner of the fax-machine stand. "About that. I was late for work this morning and I have a half hour to make up. What time does the day care close again?"

"Funny. I'll let you have the half hour, but just this once." He heard papers rattling on her end and people talking in the background. It was an hour earlier where she was, and she no doubt had skipped out of a meeting so she could check on him. "I'll call you later to say good night to Olivia."

"What about me?" he asked.

He could tell she was smiling by the tone of her voice. "I suppose I could say good night to you, too."

He hung up the phone, the silly grin still on his face.

"Was that Cass?"

Logan jumped. He hadn't heard Baxter Dempsey come up to the desk. The man seemed to pop out of the woodwork sometimes.

"Yeah." He lowered his foot from the fax machine to the floor and used it to spin the chair around so he faced the other man, but he didn't stand up.

"You two have gotten close," Dempsey said. He tugged at the sleeves of his suit, a sign of irritation, even though none of it showed in his expression.

"Turns out she lives next door to my grandmother."

Behind Dempsey, Logan saw a few of the braver staff begin to trickle out early. The rest would be watching the clock, ready to dash for the exit as soon as it was safe.

"One might wonder if that creates a conflict of interest," Dempsey added.

"Really?" Logan asked. "For Cass, or my grandmother?"

"You know what I mean."

"No," he said, "I don't think I do." He kept his voice low so as not to be overheard. Plus, low was more effective. He wasn't this guy's employee, and he wasn't easily intimidated.

Dempsey stayed where he was. Logan waited patiently, curious what it was that he wanted. The trickle of workers became a full-fledged stream that parted in the center of the room, some people flowing for the stairs, others dammed at the door of the overworked elevator.

The door slid closed on the last of the staff, leaving the two men alone in the reception area.

"I hear you lost a webcam this morning," Dempsey said.

Someone in the department had reported it to him.

Logan wondered who the other man was keeping tabs on—him, or Cass. Dempsey might have no authority over him, but he did over her—and Logan hadn't forgotten how he'd threatened her job.

"Software and all," Logan replied.

Dempsey got straight to the real point. "Is Cass under investigation?"

His bold directness caught Logan off guard. "You know I can't discuss that with you."

"Then let me do the talking," Dempsey said. "I'm concerned about her. A few people in the department have complained to Human Resources about being passed over for her position and claim she's not qualified. That means I hear things all the time that I'd rather not deal with. For instance, I heard you drove her to the airport this morning. That could be taken as an abuse of authority on her part. You're here as an administrative assistant, not her personal chauffeur. She was never that friendly with her regular admin, as people have made sure to tell me. She's young, Logan. It's obvious, at least to me, that someone in the department has it in for her because of it. Any careless handling of those missing files by her department is going to land at her door, and there won't be anything I can do to help her. The company will let her go as part of their assurance to the customer that they're dealing with the problem. She doesn't really understand how office politics work yet, but I'm betting you do. I'm asking you to make sure that if she's not a part of your investigation, you don't put her in a position that can create more problems for her with Kramer Aerospace. While you're at it, don't make any trouble for yourself. A relationship with someone you're investigating can't look good on you either."

Dempsey tapped his knuckles on the reception counter for emphasis, giving Logan time to digest what he'd said, then walked away. He gave Logan a brief wave of his hand before getting into the elevator.

Logan slumped back in his chair and wondered if he'd been threatened or if Dempsey's concern for Cass genuine. Maybe he was jealous.

Or perhaps was he deflecting attention off something — or somebody — else.

He asked himself if it was worth the expense to have Dempsey placed under surveillance, too, but decided against it. The VP had already been vetted once. Having him tailed would be difficult to justify without a good reason, and Logan was honest. He didn't want any negative light cast on Cass, and it pained him to admit that Dempsey was right about their relationship and how it would be perceived. He'd hoped to protect Cass, not hurt her.

He eyed his watch and realized he had to get moving or he'd never reach the daycare before his five twenty deadline. And he was willing to bet that Cass would call him at five twenty-one.

...

Logan and Olivia were waiting for Cass when she got off her 8:00 p.m. flight.

She spotted them through the glass wall as she came down the escalator toward the baggage-claim area, Logan tall and utterly gorgeous, Olivia pink and adorable in his arms. Others had noticed them, too. No normal woman could ignore a handsome man holding a baby, and she was as susceptible as anyone, especially when the baby was hers. She couldn't help the happy thrill of anticipation that shot through her, not all of which had to do with seeing her daughter after three difficult days away from her.

Logan was oblivious to all the attention. He'd spotted Cass and was pointing her out to Olivia—who remained insultingly distracted by the bright lights and confusion around her and didn't seem to care that her mommy was home.

Cass tried to smooth her hair. She'd gone straight to the airport when her business dinner had finished. Her skirt was wrinkled, curls had escaped from her ponytail clip, and her lipstick was long gone. That there were circles under her eyes went without saying. She wished she didn't look as if she'd just crawled off a plane after three days of meetings where her department's performance had been under intense government scrutiny.

All in all, she thought the sessions had gone well. She was tired but also relieved, as if a great weight had been lifted. A warm glow filled her heart. It helped to be welcomed home by the two people she most wanted to see. She'd missed them both.

The security doors at the base of the escalator stairs slid apart, and she wheeled her hand luggage into the baggage-claim area.

Logan met her partway. She wondered how she should greet him in public—with a handshake, a polite kiss on the cheek, or something more demonstrative—but he didn't seem as enthusiastic to see her as she'd expected, and she hesitated too long and the moment was lost. He took the extension handle of her bag in his free hand.

"How was your flight?" he asked, a distance in his manner that hadn't been there when she left.

Since she'd been the one who'd wanted to keep her personal life private, she had no idea why it bothered her that he seemed willing to comply.

"Fine," she said.

Someone jostled her from behind, and confused, she stepped to the side to give them room to get by. Then she reached for Olivia, as anxious to hold her as she was in need of a distraction.

Olivia turned away, hiding her face against Logan. Cass, stunned by this second and far more painful rejection, felt as if her heart had been dashed to the terminal floor and stepped on by a stranger's careless heel.

Logan juggled Olivia and the hand luggage. His blue eyes came alive with compassion and kind reassurance, nudging out some of the reserve.

"This is perfectly normal, Cass," he said, speaking over Olivia's mop of dark chocolate ringlets. "Babies are like cats. They pay attention to whoever's been feeding them.

My nephews did this to their mother all the time when they were little and she'd been away. Olivia's tired and she's gotten used to me. Give her a second to readjust."

Cass was tired, too, but she didn't do crying—especially in public—even if this wasn't the warm welcome she'd foolishly anticipated.

The baggage carrousel with her flight number on it jerked to life. People surged forward to crowd around.

"Come on," Logan said. "Let's find your luggage and get out of here."

A half hour later, when they'd gotten Olivia and the luggage stored in the minivan and were on their way home, things inched back to normal. Cass had finally been granted a slobbery kiss from her daughter, and all was right on that end.

Logan remained too preoccupied for easy company. Cass shifted in the passenger seat, pretending to check on her daughter in the back, when she was really studying him. He was normally so relaxed. Tonight, he seemed tense. Wherever they were, his thoughts weren't with her.

"Did you have any trouble with Olivia?" she asked.

The first stars twinkled in a darkening, azure evening sky. Streetlights marked their route with puddles of yellow. He took the ramp leading onto the highway, then cut into traffic.

The muscles in his jaw relaxed as he smiled at the windshield.

"Not at all. We had pizza and beer every night and stayed up until midnight watching mixed martial arts in your bedroom. She can really hold her liquor." He slid a sideways glance at Cass, taking his eyes off the road for a fraction of a second. "Yet another way in which she takes after her mother."

This was more like it.

"Watching mixed martial arts might be good for her," Cass said. "She should learn to take care of herself."

"Especially if she decides to challenge your record and hitchhike across the entire country, not just half of it." He risked another sly glance in her direction, then turned serious. "I know it was hard for you to leave her with me, especially since you don't know me very well. Thank you for that."

"It was hard leaving her, period. Leaving her with you wasn't difficult at all." Not after she'd seen the way he looked at Olivia.

It wasn't a handsome man with a baby that she found so irresistible, she discovered with a jolt of awareness. It was Logan with theirs. He loved Olivia, or was starting to. There was no question about that. And it was immensely appealing.

She had liked him from the moment she'd set eyes on him. She'd wanted him, although at the time in a sexual way, not an emotional one. The other night, liking and wanting had tipped a little further into uncharted territory, at least for her, and even though they'd slept together, she wasn't quite sure how to proceed. If she were to judge by the mixed signals he sent, then he wasn't ready for anything permanent. Until he figured out what he wanted, or was willing to offer Olivia, at least, then Cass had to be the responsible adult.

She'd done okay so far.

But she wasn't comfortable dancing around the topic of Olivia any longer. For her own peace of mind, she needed to know where things between them were headed. Her heart

was already invested a little too deep.

She was going to come clean.

Traffic was light and it wasn't long before they were home. Cass collected Olivia, who was sound asleep, from her car seat, while Logan retrieved the luggage.

Inside the house, Cass flipped on the light in the entry and started for the upstairs, intending to put Olivia to bed. Logan hovered at the front door as if unsure whether or not to come in.

"Can you hang on for a few minutes?" she called to him over her shoulder. "I'd like to talk to you."

She tucked Olivia in her crib and kissed her round cheek. They'd be able to sleep late in the morning. Cass wouldn't go to the office until after lunch, so they'd have a few extra mother-and-daughter hours together.

Right now, Logan was waiting.

She took the time to strip out of her suit and switch into sweats. Not exactly her sexiest look, but she'd bought her clothes around work and motherhood, not men.

He was sprawled on the sofa in her front room with his head tipped back and his eyes closed and one arm across his stomach. His hair spiked up at the front as if he'd forked his fingers through it. The lights were off, leaving only a soft glow seeping in from the front entry and through the filmy curtains off the street. It was late, and he looked as tired as she felt. She guessed sex was off the table tonight. Taking care of a toddler alone wasn't easy, no matter how much he'd downplayed it.

She tumbled onto the sofa beside him. He opened one bleary eye.

"I have no idea how you do it," he said. "I'm exhausted."

"You get used to it, although I do admit that the first few weeks back to work after my maternity leave weren't easy ones."

He didn't move, simply watched her in the semidarkness until she had to fight not to squirm. She'd like to know what he was thinking. Somehow, she didn't think it was about getting her naked.

She hooked her fingers in his belt and hauled herself closer. The arm that had been resting on his stomach lifted, snaking along the back of the sofa to drape over her shoulders. She curled up against him, her hands under her cheek and her head on his chest. He popped the release on her hair clip like a pro and tossed it onto the end table, then ruffled her loosened curls with his fingers.

Longing unfurled in her stomach, a rabble of metamorphosing butterflies that fluttered on fresh-minted wings. She reached up with one hand to tickle the nape of his neck. She could feel his heart pounding and the way his breath caught in his throat as he kissed her.

"I missed you," he said.

She didn't want to read too much into that, so instead, simply burrowed in closer. Having someone to come home to was a first for her, and she discovered she liked it. While the sex was great, companionship at the end of a long, tiring day was worth as much, if not more.

Her own heart flipped like crazy.

"What did you want to talk to me about?" he asked.

It was now or never. She took the plunge, but could feel herself speaking too fast. "I know that what happened in Ottawa was supposed to be a one-night hookup between us—something we both could enjoy and forget—but unfortunately, that isn't how things turned out."

The room fell so silent that she could hear the pipes gurgle in the walls. Logan lifted his arm from her shoulders and put distance between them.

"Don't do this," he said.

She saw none of the usual kindness and humor in the piercing blueness of his eyes. In fact she saw nothing, because he'd shut her out.

Hurt scorched through her. She didn't want anything from him. She simply thought he deserved the truth.

They both did.

"Don't do what?" she asked.

She was going to make him come right out and say it. That he didn't want to make any commitments. She'd been fine with that once, because at the time, she'd felt the same.

A baby changed everything. At least for her.

"Don't say anything you'll regret," Logan said. "I can't explain my situation to you right now." He rubbed the back of his neck. "Please, Cass. I mean it. Not yet. I need more time."

She knew not all men made good fathers. Her own was a classic example of how not to parent. But she'd come to believe that Logan was different. All she had to do was see them together to know that he loved Olivia.

Then he'd spent caregiving time with her, and it was no longer all fun and games, and it seemed as if loving her wasn't enough. He'd discovered how much responsibility a toddler could be, and he wasn't big on that.

"When will be a better time? Five years from now? Ten? When Olivia graduates from college? What decade of her life would most suit your convenience?" She couldn't hold back her hurt any longer. It spilled over, like lava from an oozing volcano. She'd let him in, and he'd let her down. "She's your daughter, too, Logan. I thought you should know. I don't expect you to take any financial responsibility for her. I'm not asking for anything. But I also don't intend to allow you to flit in and out of her life whenever the timing happens to be good for you. Grow up and grow a pair. Either be a father to her, or leave us alone."

Cass's throat tensed, making it too painful for her to swallow, as she waited to see what he'd say or do next.

A muscle leaped in his jaw, the only sign of distress on his part.

"I should go," he said.

Chapter Thirteen

Logan had no one to blame but himself that the evening was ruined. He and Cass were both tired, and his thoughts had been on his job, not her. He'd misread all the signals.

He had no trouble reading them now. Resolve filled the cool hazel eyes staring at him with such disappointment.

"This is my own fault. I expected too much from you," Cass said. "Olivia's so wonderful I assumed you had to be, too. In my head, I made you out to be a different person than you are." She let out a light laugh. "How st-st-stupid am I? You'd think I'd have learned by now that I can't make someone be who I want. And yes. I think you should go."

Those were definitely words she'd regret. Ice water coursed through him. He had to tell her the truth, because the real lesson she'd learned from her father was how not to forgive.

A car pulled into the driveway.

Through the crack in the curtains, he could see a gray

Lexus. At first he thought it was simply turning around. Then the headlights shut off, the driver's door opened, and someone got out.

"You have company," he said.

He followed Cass to the door. It was late, and she wasn't opening the door to a stranger. He hung back a few steps, out of sight in the shadows of the front room, curious who'd be calling at this time of night.

She peered through the keyhole then unlocked the door, swinging it wide.

"David," she said with surprise.

The blind date. Her nosy friend's brother.

He was blond, expensively dressed, and drove a great car. Jealousy hit Logan like a sock full of quarters, but he shook it off. Cass wasn't interested. She wouldn't change her mind just because she was angry with Logan.

"I was driving by on my way home from Tricia's, and I saw your light on," David was saying. "Is this a bad time to drop in?"

She put a hand to her hair as if self-conscious about her appearance, and glanced down at her clothes. She had on a close-fitting white hoodie and navy sweats that displayed the long, lean line of her body and legs, and Logan thought she looked gorgeous—kind of tousled, as if she were flustered, not furious.

"I just got back from a business trip. I wasn't expecting company," she said.

Logan stepped from the darkened front room into the brightly lit entry, coming up behind her but not getting territorially close.

When David caught sight of him, a sudden rigidness

entered his stance. Logan watched him reassess the casual clothing that Cass would never have traveled for work in, meaning she'd had time to change. Her hair, too, screamed that a man's hands had recently been in it, and Logan was the only other one in the room.

David threw Cass a tight smile of embarrassment. "This *is* a bad time."

She handled the situation with dignity, as if this were a business meeting and not an awkward encounter during a fight. "David, this is Logan, one of my coworkers."

Logan stretched out his hand. The other man took it in a firm grip. The handshake lasted less than two seconds. "Pleased to meet you," he said. "I'm Cass's administrative assistant. I picked her up at the airport this evening."

"Admin assistant, huh?" The tension eased from David, although not the curiosity. "Cass a demanding boss?"

Logan couldn't resist. "She can be dominating."

Cass bit her lip but said nothing.

David's arrival gave him an easy excuse to avoid a conversation it was too early to hold. The second he left here, however, he was calling his team leader. Before he did anything else, he had to tell him about Olivia.

"I've got to be going," he said to Cass. "We'll talk tomorrow."

Her eyes tracked his movements as he walked out the door and down the front steps, taking them two at a time. He felt them burning into his back, as well as her acute disappointment in him. The door clicked shut behind him with a finality that rang in his ears.

He stopped on his grandmother's side of the break in the hedge so he could spy on her for a few minutes more.

The two shadowy figures never moved from the front foyer. He could just make them out through the narrow strip of milky glass framing the door.

A few minutes later, David left and Logan could think clearly again.

Logan strode through the night shadows sprawling across the damp, spongy lawn to his grandmother's garage. He didn't dare wait until morning to check in with his team. He should have told his team leader everything already, but he'd been too jealous of his time alone with Olivia the past few days and hadn't wanted anything taking away from the sheer joy of it.

He loved being a father.

Before he talked to Cass about Olivia, and the future, he had to know how much he could tell her about his situation. The first reports were in from the CSIS agent who'd been trailing Isabelle. So far, no unusual activity—but the grandson she'd spoken of had raised a serious red flag. Further investigating revealed that Isabelle's only son, the grandson's father, had been killed by an improvised explosive device on his first deployment in the Middle East. They'd missed it during her security clearances because her son went by a different last name. She'd never married the nonmilitary father, and the son had been raised by him and his wife. The son had followed in Isabelle's footsteps and enlisted, but he'd chosen the army, not the navy.

She'd lied on the security clearance, which in itself could get her fired, but there could be any number of personal reasons why she'd done it that had nothing to do with espionage. Her service record was clean. If he went through the security forms of everyone in the company, he'd no doubt find others who'd paid a similar, less than strict attention to the clearance requirements.

So Logan didn't yet have a case.

And even if his team leader removed him, he doubted he'd be allowed to tell Cass anything. After all, it was her department under investigation.

He hadn't forgotten that her job was in danger, either. Kramer Aerospace wasn't shunting off a longstanding problem onto someone new to the department. Not if he could help it. There was also the possibility that Dempsey was playing some sort of game.

The inside of the garage smelled of old wood and diesel, and he could hear mice in the walls and the rafters, but it was private. Logan called his team leader while he could still say with reasonable honesty that he'd only this minute found out about Olivia for sure.

"You're a dumbass," his team leader said once he'd heard Logan out. "Does Cass Stone know who you are and why you're there?"

"No."

"Then we'll have to worry about this mess later. Luckily for you, we've got a middle-aged blonde woman on the webcam program the techs retrieved from your computer. Shows her face up close and plain as day, right before the screen goes blank, and the image matches the security photo for Isabelle Walsh. That's enough to get us wiretaps and into her bank accounts, but not enough to convict her. Based on all the information you have, how confident are you that she's the one?"

Logan thought again of the grandson, and the son who'd been killed on deployment, and how people would do anything for their children. Her security clearance forms for Kramer Aerospace were three years old. The son had been dead for two—which meant he should have been listed.

Some of the pain in his chest eased. He wouldn't have to betray any of Cass's confidences. He had a solid suspect.

"Enough to put pressure on her and have her arrested," he said.

"Okay, then." He heard the team leader talking to someone else, giving them instructions. He came back on the line, speaking to Logan. "Set it up. Get her into a meeting and start asking questions. See if you can get a confession."

If she confessed, that would be easiest for everyone. Often, in similar cases, former military chose not to fight it because they knew what they faced.

They simply tried to downplay their actions to get the lightest sentence possible.

"And Logan?"

"Yes, Boss?"

"Until we get that confession, I don't want any pillow talk happening. Understood?"

No. He wanted to have that talk with Cass now. This very second.

"Understood," Logan said, and hung up.

• • •

Logan took the elevator from the conference room floor to Dempsey's office at eight o'clock sharp, nodding to the executive assistant on his way past her desk.

Over the past joyous few weeks, he'd developed an affinity for executive and administrative assistants the world over. They had to be well organized and detail-oriented, and willing to overlook people too high and mighty to send their own faxes.

He'd rather tend bar.

He took a seat across from Dempsey, who seemed tired, and maybe resigned. This was the point when people usually began searching for some kind of explanation. Often, they tried to distance themselves from the crime.

"We've got a suspect," Logan said. "Standard procedure is similar to firing an employee. She'll be called into a private meeting with you and me. When that happens, you'll want to make sure that she no longer has access to company information."

If he didn't get a confession, Isabelle would have to be put on suspension. Guilty or not, people accused of espionage tended to carry a grudge against their employers and had been known to do damage to electronic filing systems and other company property.

Dempsey remained quiet. Unnaturally so. He turned his chair so that he faced the window and the view of the harbor, as if lost in deep thought.

"I'll ask her a few questions," Logan continued, "and push her a little. If she's guilty—and I'm fairly certain she is—that should be enough to make her talk. Two officers will be sent to cover the main door so she can't slip out before the meeting. Once she's in with us I'll have them come and stand outside the room, waiting for my signal to make the arrest."

Dempsey sighed. Sounded defeated.

"Cass has always been such a good employee," he said to the window, "but she's had a lot to handle the past two years. Being a single mother, on top of a job with her level of responsibility, hasn't been easy for her. I wish she'd come to me for help, but I did all I could."

Logan had no idea what he was rambling on about. They were talking about theft of classified government information. Then, with a shock, he figured it out.

Baxter Dempsey believed Cass was guilty.

"Are you the one who's been going into Cass's office after hours and searching through her things?" Logan asked.

Dempsey turned his head to look at Logan, then spun his chair around. "Are you out of your mind? Why would I do such a thing?"

"Why would you think Cass is guilty?" Logan shot back.

"She's not?"

"Of course she isn't. Any fool could see that. One of the writers is. Isabelle Walsh."

Dempsey's face said his memory on the name drew a blank. It was plain to Logan that he had no idea who she was. "I never went into Cass's office when she wasn't in it."

"I'm fairly confident Isabelle's responsible for that, too."

Dempsey looked more confused. "Why?"

"She's gone to a great deal of trouble to make sure people think she's got a problem with Cass," he explained. "She's no doubt trying to downplay the seriousness of what she's really been doing in case she ever gets caught. That means we aren't going to include it as part of this investigation." The one classified file left on Cass's desk was all that linked the two circumstances, and it had been mixed in with files Logan had handled. If Isabelle was playing some game, he wasn't going to participate in it. He wasn't bringing Cass into it either.

"Cass needs to be here when you question Isabelle," Dempsey said. "It's her staff member and her department."

Logan didn't want her involved at all, but he could tell Dempsey wasn't going to budge. He could move the arrest somewhere else, but it involved Kramer Aerospace and he wanted to discuss improving their procedures with them. As a company, they'd followed contractual requirements and were under no obligations. He'd like to get their cooperation rather than be forced to recommend a contract review, and taking a mutual "move forward" approach meant they'd have no reason to assign blame. Cass's job would be safe.

Being able to get everything out in the open with her, and maybe impress her a little, wouldn't be such a bad thing either.

"Okay," Logan said. "Have your IT department shut down Isabelle's computer access tonight. I'll let you know when she leaves. Call Cass in early so we can debrief her. We'll meet in the fourth-floor conference room first thing in the morning."

...

He was finishing his lunch as Cass walked into the office that afternoon, briefcase in one hand and her cell phone pressed to her ear. Flicking it off with her thumb, she paused at the reception desk and peered over the counter.

"What *do* you eat?" she asked, fixing on the waxed paper wrapping he'd crumpled and tossed in the trash.

He swallowed the last mouthful of sandwich as he tried to get a bead on her mood. Reading Cass was hard for him, probably because he was too close. He hadn't exactly left her on a high note last night, so the fact she was speaking to him couldn't be good.

"That was smoked meat on rye, courtesy of Nan." He held up a half-empty bottle of apple juice. "She wouldn't pack me a beer, so I had to settle for this."

"Your grandmother makes your lunch?"

He got it now. Cass was spoiling for a fight, and any topic would do.

"Because she insists, not because I ask. I'm not total dead weight," he added. "I can take care of myself."

"I never said you couldn't take care of yourself. You seem to have no problems with that."

He could read between the lines. *Because you're a selfish bastard.*

He'd earned her negative opinion of him. That didn't make it easier to deal with. When this was over, he'd have a lot of explaining to do. He hoped she'd listen. Right now he'd do well to keep his head down and stay off her radar.

She went into her office and closed the door. A little while later he could hear the muffled sound of her voice as she spoke on the phone, presumably responding to voicemail messages.

Footsteps pattered on the floor from the direction of the writing department. Isabelle appeared, pausing in front of the ladies' room around the corner from the elevator, one hand on the door.

"Her Ladyship has returned?" she stage-whispered to Logan.

He gave her a thumbs-up, and she disappeared.

Cass came out of her office. A light flush had crept up her neck from the collar of her crisp white blouse. Judging by the guns-blazing glare in her hazel eyes, he guessed she'd found a good reason to fight.

"What on earth were you doing with a personal webcam hooked up to your computer?" she asked.

So much for keeping his head down. That must have been Baxter Dempsey she'd been talking to on the phone.

He pushed his chair back, the worn casters scraping on the tile. "Let's take this into your office."

Once they were inside, he closed the door. He couldn't tell her about the theft of the publications, but he'd had another purpose for installing the webcam that she should hear about.

"I was using the camera to monitor traffic going in and out of your office while you aren't here," he said.

"Thank you for your concern, but that wasn't necessary," she said. "Nothing's been taken and no real harm's been done."

"Except for my webcam," he felt obliged to point out.

"Really, Logan." She put her hands on her hips. "You should have known better. The reception area is wide open. Your camera could have been taken by anyone. It's a tempting little piece of equipment, and I know that people help themselves to office supplies all the time. They might have thought it belonged to the department. If anything, it was most likely someone from another floor who took it."

Cass wasn't stupid. She was young and uncertain, and unused to command. She wanted to trust the people she worked with, and he got that, so she was making excuses for them.

The truth was, there were a few bad apples in every bag. People took things from work for all kinds of reasons. Most felt entitled to them. Isabelle had already told him that staff treated the office supplies as one of the benefits of the job. That didn't make it right.

"Stealing a webcam off someone's computer goes beyond office supply theft. I can understand that you don't want to make any unnecessary trouble around here," he added, "but your job is probationary right now so you should be thinking more about protecting yourself. Someone's messing with you. Go with your gut. Off the top of your head, give me two names."

"How do you know my job is probationary?" she asked.

Her question threw him off. As usual, she zeroed in on something not relevant to the conversation at hand, but of considerable significance overall.

He scrabbled through his memory for a good answer and came up blank. "You told me."

Her eyes narrowed. "No I didn't."

He shrugged. "I must have heard it around the office."

"Nice. Whoever you heard it from is probably one of the two names you want, then. Personally, I can't think of anyone." She tapped the toe of her shoe against the leg of her desk, an inconsequential movement she seemed unaware of that told him she was under stress. She frowned. "I know you're trying to help, but accusing the staff of theft isn't the best way to do it."

"That's why I thought the webcam was the right way to go," he said.

She gave him a look of pinch-mouthed displeasure. He wasn't often intimidated by authority, but he had to admit, she had a way of making him squirm. "Spying on them isn't good either."

"Wouldn't you rather I look like the bad guy, not you? I don't have to work here much longer." He folded his arms and rocked on his heels. "You, as you already pointed out, are stuck."

"Everyone will think you were doing something I told you to do," she said. She rubbed her temples as if her head ached.

"I'm sorry, Cass," he said, and meant it. "For everything."

"I don't get you." She sighed. "We need to talk about Olivia. I didn't want to do this at work, but I don't want you in my house anymore, so we'll have to do it here."

That really hurt. But he'd been told not to say anything about the investigation to her.

"I want Olivia," he said. "I want you both."

"Really?" she asked. "What are your plans once Theresa comes back? Is the Caribbean still on?"

"I thought I might stick around here instead." It felt great to be able to tell her the truth on that much, at least. He had been planning on staying. Cornwall was nice. He'd loved it as a kid. They'd take things slow. She could use the child support he owed her to finish fixing her house. He could help with the repairs.

He had an entire fantasy happening in his head when he suddenly realized he should have been paying attention.

"You do what you have to," she was saying. "But I have Olivia to think of, and I need to do what's best for her. Don't include us in your plans."

"Just like that, you're cutting me out?" The thought of never seeing Olivia again ripped out his heart.

"Just like that?" she echoed. "You walked out on me last night. How many more chances am I supposed to give you?"

"One," he said, trying to breathe past the pain.

"Then tell me why today, all of a sudden, everything's changed."

"Nothing's changed. I wanted you both last night. I want you both now."

"And I don't believe you. So convince me."

"One more day, Cass. Please."

"I don't think so." Her eyes puddled with tears, but she blinked them back. Other than that, her gaze remained steady. Her voice firm. No telltale little stutter. "I offered you the one secret that's more important to me than anything, and you chose not to accept it."

He weighed his options. He wanted to tell her everything right then and there, and the hell with what his team leader said, because she needed someone to put her first for a change. In her whole life, she'd never had anyone do that for her.

He'd be the first. From this point on, she'd know who she could count on.

"Excuse me," Cass said, her voice cool and distant. "We both have work to do."

She turned back to her desk.

Logan lost his ability to speak. He swung his mouth closed. She'd dismissed him as if he were a poorly performing employee. Like some guy serving her drinks in a bar.

And then it was his turn to be pissed. He was good at his job. Responsible. Let her see it for herself. After that, she could judge him.

He closed the office door behind him on his way out.

Chapter Fourteen

The rest of Cass's day passed in a blur. She was busy catching up, she was tired from her trip and a poor night's sleep, and to top it all off, she had to go into work early in the morning for a meeting that Baxter said couldn't wait.

By the time she entered the daycare to take Olivia home, she was able to put the whole situation with Logan into perspective.

She'd been stupid to let him in. She should have gone with her first instincts and kept him away from Olivia, although really, it hardly mattered. He didn't want his daughter. He didn't want Cass either. If he did, he'd have made more of an effort when he had the chance. She shouldn't have to force him to take action.

She was on the sidewalk in front of the daycare, fastening Olivia into the stroller, when her friend Patricia's BMW purred up to the curb. There was no immediate parking available, so she waved for Cass to come closer.

Patricia's flat-ironed, platinum-blond hair caught on a breeze and she brushed it away from her face, holding it back with one hand. "David said he dropped by your house on his way home last night."

Cass had completely forgotten. He hadn't stayed. He'd asked her if she'd like to go for a drink again sometime, she'd said no thanks, and that was the end of it. Or so she'd thought.

"I'd just gotten back from three days of meetings in Ottawa," she said. "I was beat."

Patricia waved off the excuse. A faint, knowing smile touched her glossy-pink lips as she shifted the BMW into park. "You aren't obligated to date my brother, Cass. I like you and hoped you'd both hit it off. But he said your administrative assistant was with you when he arrived, and he felt as if he'd interrupted something. Would this admin assistant be the same hottie who's been taking Olivia back and forth to daycare while you were away? The one I saw sitting on your front doorstep last week?"

"I don't know what you're talking about," Cass said.

"Save it." Patricia saw a parking space open up as one of the other parents drove off. "Hang on a sec."

She maneuvered her car into the vacated space, and then slid her long legs from the car. She walked toward Cass, smoothed the back of her narrow skirt, and crouched on her heels so she could say hi to Olivia, tousling Olivia's curls, before returning her attention to Cass.

The big smile she'd been wearing reappeared. "Okay, now tell me why the hottie admin assistant has been acting more like a personal one. And I want details."

Patricia had no idea she was pouring salt on an open

and festering wound. Cass might like to keep her feelings to herself, but she wasn't without them.

"There aren't any," she said. "I already told you. He works in my office. His grandmother lives next door and he's been staying with her. Having him handle daycare duty while I was away was a convenience. That's it."

Patricia arched an eyebrow. "You didn't say anything about him working for you. And I find it surprising that you'd leave Olivia for three days with a man you claim there aren't any details about simply because his grandmother lives next door to you."

"He took Olivia back and forth to d-d-daycare." She felt her cheeks start to burn. It wasn't a lie, simply not the whole truth.

"You're a terrible liar," Patricia said. "But okay. We'll pretend I believe you. That doesn't explain why Olivia calls him Daddy."

Cass was torn between confusion and a blinding, murderous rage. He had the nerve to call her Dr. Jekyll and Mrs. Hyde, and then he did things like this. She struggled for a reasonable explanation.

"He thinks he's funny," she managed to say.

"Really?" Patricia's face echoed her doubt. "It seemed to me as if he adores her. You should see the way his face lights up when he talks about her."

Cass had seen the look so she knew what Patricia meant, but she didn't want to hear this right now. She didn't like feeling hurt and confused. She'd rather be angry with Logan. He'd fooled her, so it shouldn't be a surprise that he'd fooled others, too.

Patricia wasn't finished, and Cass's silence didn't stop

her. "You said you're ready to meet men. Maybe you're ready to meet the right man, and not just anyone. So what's wrong with him, Cass? And don't tell me there's no attraction because we'll both know you're lying. I think he's incredibly hot, and I'm happily married."

Cass's cheeks blistered with heat. "There's nothing wrong with him." Not that she wanted to talk about. She could hardly say he was commitment-phobic without getting into his relationship to Olivia.

That wasn't going to happen.

"I know I'm interfering," Patricia persisted, "but if it's because he works for you, then do something about it. Have him transferred to another department. Or is this about the fact you make more money than he does?"

She seized on that point so she could end the conversation. "He lacks ambition."

"I don't believe you. If you were only interested in success, you'd be more willing to give David a chance. I may be his sister and somewhat prejudiced, but I still know he's a catch." Patricia waved to the daycare worker trying to catch her attention. "I've got to get Frankie. Quit worrying what other people think, Cass. If you want him, go after him."

Patricia dashed off with a final tug on Olivia's curls, and Cass turned the stroller up the sidewalk toward home, thinking about the well-intentioned advice and how her friend had it all wrong.

She didn't worry about other people's opinions, only her own. And right now, what she thought about Logan wasn't very flattering to him.

. . .

Logan had called in sick the next morning, so to find him waiting with Baxter in the conference room when Cass arrived came as a surprise.

The glaring fluorescent lights caught the faint shadow of dark beard he could never seem to rid himself of, and made his eyes look as blue as the fresh paint on the walls.

Nervous anxiety burned in her stomach when she saw him seated at the head of the table. Something was wrong.

Baxter pulled out a chair on Logan's right and motioned for her to take the one on the left, across from him. The long table seated twelve.

"What's going on?" she asked, sitting uncomfortably straight and folding her hands in her lap. She felt much as she had the one time she'd been called to the principal's office for cutting class.

Baxter hurried to reassure her. "Not what you think. Logan's going to explain."

Cass found she couldn't look at him without the fiery rage she thought she'd conquered reigniting.

"Someone's been stealing classified information from your department and selling it to foreign agents," Logan said. "I was assigned to find out who it is."

His words were bewildering and difficult to process past all her pent-up emotions. When they did register, she couldn't quite believe their inference.

"Assigned by whom?" she asked Baxter.

"Logan is CSIS, Cass," Baxter said.

One by one, all of the pieces clicked into place. He'd been investigating her and her department. Not much wonder she and Olivia had been such a huge inconvenience for him. He hadn't refused to acknowledge Olivia because he was afraid of commitment. He'd chosen not to acknowledge her because she'd get in the way of his job. It had to be hard, trying to get to know his daughter when her mother might be a thief.

At least he'd had full access to Cass's entire private life, as well as her background. That had to be a big help to him. Her cheeks burned with simmering anger. She'd told him things about herself that nobody else knew. She'd thought she loved him, but it turned out he was as much a stranger now as he had been in Ottawa.

She knew nothing about him, other than that he had to be good at his job to have fooled her so completely. She was left feeling any number of things, but mostly stupid, naive, and manipulated.

She tried to pay attention while he explained about one of the writers, and why he thought Isabelle Walsh was guilty, which should have come as a relief, but made her angrier instead. Her hands wouldn't stop shaking so she clenched them as tight as she could. Big deal. She was innocent by elimination.

Consequently, she almost missed one critical piece of information. She dragged her attention back to the meeting.

"Why would Isabelle keep leaving my office unlocked?" she asked.

"I'm sure she was doing a lot more than that. However, that's not part of this investigation," Logan said. "If she brings it up, even in passing, please don't respond. While I'm questioning her it's best if you both listen but don't try to participate. Her conversation will be with me."

Someone knocked on the door, a light tap that nevertheless gave Cass a start.

Baxter got up to open it.

"Come in," he said to Isabelle.

• • •

Logan watched as Isabelle took note of everyone in the room and saw the flash of awareness that told him she knew she'd been found out.

He had her. This would be easier than he'd hoped.

But she wasn't going down easily.

"I was told Human Resources wanted to see me." She looked from Logan to Dempsey. "If this is about the office supplies, really. I can't be the only person in the company who takes them."

"I'm not interested in the office supplies." Logan pointed to a chair beside Dempsey. He didn't believe Isabelle was dangerous, and still, he discovered he didn't want her close to Cass. It made him uneasy, and too aware of Cass, and right now he needed to focus on his job. "Please sit down."

Isabelle sat. She folded her hands and rested them on the table. All the while, she maintained an air of innocence that he wasn't buying. Her body language was all wrong. If she were indeed innocent, she'd be showing more outward signs of distress. She'd be anxious. Nobody liked ugly surprises, and Isabelle knew full well that this was about as ugly as it got.

"I've been brought in to investigate the theft of classified information from Kramer Aerospace, and its sale to foreign agents," he said, then waited.

Isabelle's clasped knuckles whitened, yet her eyes remained open wide as she tried to convey innocence.

She was definitely guilty.

The silence in the room threatened to stretch to infinity. This was the uncomfortable part for most people, but Cass and Dempsey did nothing to break it.

"You're CSIS, aren't you?" Isabelle said. "And you think it was me because I told you I helped myself to a few office supplies?"

"I think it was you because your face shows up on my computer while you're stealing my webcam," he replied. "And because you lied on your security clearance about your next of kin. Your son, by the way, would be ashamed of you right now. You're a veteran. This is no way to respect one of our fallen soldiers. Especially not your own son."

"My son wouldn't have anything to do with me," Isabelle said. "That's why he's not listed. He didn't mind asking me to take care of his kid before his last deployment because his girlfriend walked out on them, though. Try raising a family on military benefits."

She sounded bitter and angry, not at all like a loving grandparent, and he felt sorry for the boy. While his own was quite stable and ordinary, through his work he'd seen all kinds of dysfunctional families. Some people coped better than others. Cass had a messed-up one too, as well as a baby to care for, and she hadn't resorted to espionage. Most people didn't.

Isabelle had brought up the subject of money on her own. He hadn't mentioned the recent boosts to her bank account, so she was already on the defensive. That was good.

He spread a palm on the table and leaned back in the padded conference chair. "I'm not here to judge. I am curious, though, where the large amount of money in your account came from, especially if pensions are so inadequate."

"If you're looking for people to accuse based on circumstantial evidence," Isabelle said, "then why not check out Cass's situation? She's got a baby with no father. And what about Baxter, here? Rumor has it the baby is his. Hiding child support from his wife has got to be hard."

Cass drew in a sharp breath of shock, and Dempsey looked stunned. Both succeeded in keeping their opinions to themselves.

Logan had already heard the gossip, so he didn't waste a response. He already knew who the father was. "We aren't talking about them. We're talking about you."

"Am I being charged with anything?" Isabelle asked. "If so, I want to speak with a lawyer."

The interview was over. Logan punched a button on the speaker phone in the center of the table and asked for the two agents to be sent in.

Half an hour later, he was once again alone with Cass and Dempsey.

He spoke to Dempsey about what staff would be told. He asked for, and got, permission to review company procedures for handling classified publications.

Then he turned to Cass. She seemed completely unflustered, which he knew meant something was seriously wrong. The quieter she got, the more scared he became.

It was time to get everything out in the open.

"Can I speak to you alone for a moment?" he asked.

"Is it about our procedures?" she asked.

"No."

"Then I'm a-f-f-fraid not."

She got up and left the room.

This, Logan thought, was the mother of all uncomfortable

silences.

"Sucks to be you," Dempsey said, a faint smirk on his face. Then he left, too.

Chapter Fifteen

Logan peered through the black mesh of the screen door into Cass's bright kitchen. He'd waited until he knew Olivia would be in bed. As much as he wanted to see her, right now, he needed to speak with Cass more.

"Please let me in," he said. "We need to talk."

She didn't move, simply stood there hugging her chest, looking so adorable in those ridiculous bunny slippers that his heart clenched with longing.

But she looked angry, too. And hurt, to be more specific, and that ate at his conscience. He had to make her understand that he'd had no choice but to keep secrets from her. He'd done his best to protect her and Olivia, and keep his investigation aboveboard and on track, and he'd had to sacrifice a few professional ethics to do so.

"You had plenty of opportunities for talking," she said. "Instead, you used your time with me and my daughter to nose around in my life, you lying, selfish bastard."

He blinked. "Is that what you think?"

"Am I right?" she demanded.

"Yes," he admitted, "but it wasn't for the investigation. I used any time I had with you and *our* daughter to get to know you both better. That's it. That's all I did." It might not be the best time to admit he'd snooped around in her tablet. Or ever. He shifted his stance. A sprinkle of rain dampened the back of his neck, and he jiggled the handle on the door. "Let me in. Just for a few minutes. If you don't like what I have to say, I'll leave and never come back."

Which was a complete lie, because he'd come back as many times as he had to. Right now he'd do or say whatever it took to get him inside.

She grasped the inner door and any second, he expected to have it slammed in his face. She stood with her hand on it, her expression unreadable. Then she reached for the latch on the screen. "You've got five minutes."

He pushed it open before she could change her mind.

The kitchen was warm and smelled of roast beef. A mop and a bucket were propped against a wall. She was doing her cooking and cleaning. There were no signs she'd been sitting around missing him the way he'd been missing her.

She wouldn't, he thought. Cass carried on.

For some reason that rankled, and the first words out of his mouth weren't the ones he'd intended to say.

"Did you try to reach me when you found out you were pregnant?" he asked.

"I did."

She couldn't look him in the eye as she spoke though, and that left him wondering how hard. All the hurt over Olivia came surging back. Cass wasn't the only victim in this.

She'd had two years to adjust to being a parent. He'd only had a few weeks.

"When I walked into your department that first morning, you pretended not to know me," he said. "There was your chance, and you didn't take it. You saw someone who didn't measure up to your standards and you dismissed me. If we're also measuring who kept the bigger secret, and for the least honorable reason, then I'd have to say you. You've had Olivia to yourself for almost two years. Don't shut me out of her life again."

"You thought I was guilty of espionage."

Logan understood. She prided herself on never having done anything illegal, not even as a teenager rebelling against an autocratic father. She'd survived by using her brains then, and she'd continue to do so.

She didn't like that Logan, someone she'd trusted with her background, thought she was a criminal.

"I never thought that about you," he said. "Not for a second. I had faith in the woman I met in Ottawa who couldn't tell a good lie. I tried to protect you, as much as I could. Yet even though you trusted me enough to hook up for one night, I wasn't good enough to be Olivia's father." He couldn't get past that either.

"Are you seriously turning this around on me?" she asked. She glanced at her watch, shiny and silver on her slender wrist. "Because your time's running out."

"I'm not turning anything around on anyone. This isn't only a matter of trust. It's also a question of values." His throat tightened up and he tried to swallow to loosen it. "I did everything humanly possible to show you I could be a good father. A *great* father," he corrected himself. "I told you I needed more time. I shouldn't have had to do any more than that, yet you couldn't give me the benefit of the doubt the way I did for you. Who I am as a person should carry more weight than what I do for a living."

He watched as she pondered his words, rolling them around in her head. Some of her hostility abated, but not all. "I tried to tell you about Olivia, but whenever I brought it up you changed the subject. You made it very clear you weren't ready to hear it. You put your work first." Her voice shook as she spoke. So did her hands. She tucked them beneath her arms, as if physically trying to contain everything she was feeling. "What was I supposed to think? What am I supposed to think now?"

There it was, the real reason she was angry. Her father had refused to have anything to do with Olivia, and she'd never forgive him for it. She'd never forgive Logan for it either.

"You're supposed to trust me. To have faith in me, based on what you know about who I am. I *told* you I needed more time. Repeatedly." He rubbed the back of his neck. "My nephews will never know their father because someone like Isabelle made extra money off classified information. He was shot down in Afghanistan based on stolen intelligence. Olivia's going to have plenty of time to know hers. I'd like other children to have the same opportunity."

"I'm sorry about your nephews," she said. "But you can't just walk in here as someone I've never met before and expect me to trust you when you've never been honest with me about anything."

"You've always trusted yourself. You said you'd built me into someone different in your head. Have you considered the possibility you might have been right about me?"

She sighed as if she'd given up—that he'd worn her down—which wasn't his goal. "What do you want from me, Logan? How do we move forward from this?"

"I don't want to be shut out again. I want to be a part of Olivia's life." He took a deep breath. "I want to be a part of yours, too. I know you aren't ready to hear this, and I'm prepared to wait until you are. I'll give you all the time you need. But I love you, Cass. I fell in love with you in that bar in Ottawa when you told me you were out on parole. You were funny and smart, and so beautiful I couldn't believe my good luck. We weren't ready for each other then, and I missed my chance. I'm not missing it again."

The ice she'd wrapped around herself thinned, then cracked, giving Logan a sliver of hope.

"What were you doing in that bar in the first place?" she asked.

"It was a national defense conference full of industry members. I was working a case." He gave her a half smile, not sure how she'd take that. "I picked up that you were celebrating something because I was, too. I'd closed a file on someone who'd been selling weapons systems to hostile governments."

"People actually do things like that?"

She was so naive in so many ways, and he loved that about her. Cass's moral compass pointed true north.

"Yes, they really do." He rubbed his chin. The stubble itched, and he needed a shave, but he'd left it because he knew she liked it and had hoped it might earn him subliminal points. "Most of the time my work is dull. It's hardly dangerous. It's always confidential. So I want to be a part of your life, and Olivia's—but if you do let me in, you'll have to understand that I'm always going to be a bartender or a car salesman, or someone's administrative assistant. I know how important an education and a good job are to you," he added. "I have them. But they aren't the whole me."

He'd done all he could, and said all he could think of, at least for right now. He'd followed desperate men through dark alleys with less fear for the consequences.

Logan waited, anxious and a bit nauseous, to see how she'd react.

...

He made her sound like such a snob.

Cass couldn't say he was 100 percent wrong, and she'd make no apologies for it. She'd worked hard for everything she had. If he wanted her to accept certain things about him, he'd have to do the same for her.

"Those are important things for me to have, not someone else. Not you. I tried homelessness when I was fifteen and didn't like it a lot. Living in my father's house was only marginally better," she said. "Getting an education was my means of escape. But it's always been my opinion of myself, and my achievements, that's been most important to me. Until Olivia came along."

It was true. Once she'd left home for good, she'd had no one's opinion to worry about but her own.

"Olivia changes everything," she continued. "It's bad enough that her birth certificate lists her father as unknown. Having to explain the reason for it to her isn't a conversation I look forward to."

Logan's face paled a shade beneath the dark scruff on his jaw. "You listed me as unknown?"

"I wasn't sure of your real name," she pointed out. "I called the hotel and no one knew who you were. What else was I supposed to do? Have her go looking for someone someday who doesn't exist?"

The pain pinching his brow drove home that she wasn't without her share of secrets. She could have tried harder to find him. Pretending she hadn't wanted to create a financial burden for him had been an excuse.

She'd been afraid of rejection.

He quickly recovered. "I understand. I really do. We're both going to have a lot of explaining to do though, because believe me, my family will be asking questions long before Olivia does."

"What will you tell them?"

"That we met when we were both working in Ottawa, which is the truth. No one needs details. Those are between you and me. And that I fell for you. Hard."

The last scraps of her anger seeped away like the air from a leaky balloon, leaving her empty and deflated. She was more like her father than she'd thought. He couldn't forgive either, but this was one trait they had in common that she refused to accept. He couldn't forgive because he didn't want to. She did. She could change. Olivia deserved to have a father who loved her.

Cass deserved to be loved, too. But Logan was going to have to make some concessions if he wanted hers in return.

"I hate your job," she said. "We'll need to set boundaries. I don't like all the secrecy. And I have my own career to think about."

"We'll work something out. I'll ask for a transfer. I'm not asking you to give up your life. I'm asking you to let me in."

When she'd first met him, Cass had trusted her instincts, and it had turned into one of the best nights of her life. She'd gotten her daughter from it, and that was another thing she could never regret. He'd suggested she trust herself now.

"I said terrible things to you."

His face gentled. His voice was kind. "You said them to some loser who couldn't make a commitment. That guy wasn't me."

He was standing in her kitchen, looking at her as if she held the key to his happiness, and she made a discovery. This really was about more than Olivia to him. Cass could have happiness too, if she wanted.

She went with her instincts and followed her heart.

"I never c-c-cared that you were a bartender," she said.

Logan reached for her, and she fell into the enveloping warmth of his arms because her legs needed support. His hold on her tightened and she sank against him, resting her cheek on his shoulder. He felt solid and good.

"You really are a terrible liar. You stutter when you're trying to hide how you feel."

She smiled against him, where he couldn't see. "Okay, I cared a little."

"You only approached me because you thought you'd never see me again."

"That's true, too." She slid her hands beneath his shirt, pressing them against the small of his back, and hugged him. "But I came back to the bar because you made me a virgin."

He laughed. "That's right. The drink. You were going to get yourself into trouble with the light colonel."

"Instead, I got into trouble with you." She tipped her head back so she could look into his eyes. They were filled with the same warmth and humor she'd seen that first night she met him, and she felt the same hot rush of attraction, only this time, she felt something more. "I've never regretted it, Logan. Not even after I found out I was pregnant. Every time Olivia smiles at me, I see you. You look exactly alike."

"She has your temper." The laughter slipped from his face. "We'll be changing that birth certificate, Miss Mary. I'm adopting Olivia." He bent his head and kissed her forehead. "Do you think you could learn to love me, even if I'm never going to be someone you can talk to your coworkers and friends about?"

"You've got Ivan sending his own faxes at work," she said. "That's a pretty impressive accomplishment. The entire office has been buzzing about it."

"Be still, my heart. Your sweet talk overwhelms me with its passion."

"Bear with me. I've never had anyone tell me they love me before," she said. "We weren't a demonstrative family."

The confession embarrassed her. Olivia was never going to doubt that her mother loved her. Her father either, because Logan seemed to have no problem displaying affection.

He kissed her, his mouth warm and firm and delicious. Cass kissed him back, her heart pounding like crazy.

"Are we game for a little domination?" he asked when they came up for air, with such hope in his voice that she had to smile.

"How about role-playing?" she suggested. "The department director and the spy?"

His expression went from teasing to something more serious. "That was a question, Miss Mary. I believe you now owe me a secret."

"You asked me questions first," she objected.

He rubbed his chin along the underside of her jaw, tickling her neck and giving her such a rush of pure pleasure she almost forgot what they were talking about.

Almost, but not quite.

"You've got to be quicker than that. You missed your chance to capitalize. Now it's my turn. Do you think you can learn to love me? If only for Olivia's sake?" he asked, and Cass's heart melted.

He lied for a living, and he was way better at it than she'd ever be, but on this one particular thing, she'd never doubt him. He loved Olivia.

And he loved Cass, too.

"No," she said. She saw disappointment and hurt beginning to rise in his eyes, and rushed to stop it. "I already love you. And not for Olivia's sake, but my own."

"You won't be sorry," he said. "I'll be the best partner and father you could ever imagine."

He would be, too. Now that she understood why he'd sometimes have to keep his work to himself, what she cared most about was gaining access to everything else—because he was right. He did have a lot more to him than his job.

She'd like to think that she did, too.

"I love you," she said. This time, the words were easier to say. They swelled inside her, and made her feel somehow more complete, rather than less, when she released them. Her eyes widened as another thought occurred to her. "Olivia and I are going to have a family."

He didn't laugh. Instead, she read complete understanding in his face, as well as reassurance. He didn't need to be told how important this was to her, even though she'd only this second discovered it for herself.

"Yes, you are," he said. "What's mine is yours. You're going to love them, too. And they'll love you."

"As long as they love Olivia."

"Are you kidding? My grandmother's going to go nuts. She already likes you better than me. And she's just for starters."

Logan drew Cass close, his palms on her shoulder blades, his elbows crooked against her ribs, and he kissed her forehead, then her cheek, then nuzzled her throat. She caught her breath.

"I have plenty more secrets to share with you," she said, reaching for his hands. "But you'll have to come upstairs with me if you want to learn them."

His eyes, brilliant blue and locked on hers, were filled with fun, anticipation, and more than a hint of promise.

"Lead the way, Miss Mary. I'm yours."

About the Author

Paula Altenburg lives in rural Nova Scotia, Canada, with her husband and two sons. Once a manager in the aerospace industry, she now enjoys the luxury of working from home and writing full-time. Paula also co-authors paranormal romance under the pseudonym Taylor Keating. Visit her at www.paulaaltenburg.com.

Other Books by Paula Altenburg

DESIRE BY DESIGN

Famous architect Matt Brison is unsatisfied with his mundane life in Toronto. So when the mayor of Halifax asks him to spearhead his City Hall project, Matt jumps at the opportunity. There's just one problem: the feisty and beautiful project lead, Eve, isn't exactly thrilled about her new "coworker" hijacking her design. But when the sparks begin to fly, they both find themselves falling for the colleague they shouldn't want. And before they know it, their already shaky foundation might come crumbling down…

The Demon Outlaw Series

THE DEMON'S DAUGHTER

BLACK WIDOW DEMON

THE DEMON LORD

THE DEMON CREED

Made in the USA
Charleston, SC
12 September 2014